金融英語閱讀

(第二版)

主　編◎周婧玥
副主編◎尹　麗

前 言

　　目前大學院校的金融英語相關課程對於培養具有國際競爭力的人才有著極大的作用，它融合了英語與金融的語言和知識，對於學生來說，完全掌握是有一定的難度。而本教材是以金融英語閱讀及習題的方式，配合本科金融英語教材的需要編寫的，教材閱讀選材主要來源於近兩年一些主要英語類財經新聞、評論和書籍，內容涵蓋了金融市場到金融時事的各個方面，與現實生活息息相關，新穎實用，更能引起學生的學習興趣，注重於培養學生的語言技巧，是輔助型教材。

　　本書共有五個主題：其一是金融市場和貨幣相關的閱讀內容，包括了金融市場的概述、金融市場的歷史和金融市場的發展趨勢；其二是銀行方面的閱讀內容，包括了中央銀行、商業銀行、貨幣政策與監管的相關閱讀材料；其三是投資相關的閱讀材料，具體包括了投資銀行、債券、證券和金融衍生產品的相關閱讀內容；其四是金融行業中不可缺少的保險部分，閱讀內容包括了保險的概述、人身保險和非人身保險部分；其五是金融熱門專題，選取了當下大家關心的金融時事報導作為閱讀材料。通過對這五個部分的閱讀，讀者便可掌握和鞏固相關的金融英語術語和語言。本書第一、二、三章由周婧玥老師編寫；第四、五章由尹麗老師編寫。

　　在本書的編寫過程中，雖然前後花費了較多時間查閱編譯，但限於編者理論水平和實踐經驗的欠缺，書中難免有紕漏和不足之處，還望廣大讀者和專家予以批評指正，這將是我們繼續提高水平的絕佳機會。

編者

Table of Contents

Chapter One: Financial Market and Money ········· (1)

   Part One - Financial Market ········· (1)

      The Introduction to the Financial Market ········· (1)

      A Short History of Modern Finance ········· (5)

   Part Two - The Trend of the Financial Market ········· (9)

      Brokerage Firms Move to Set Up Futures Markets ········· (9)

   Part Three - Money ········· (12)

Chapter Two: Banking System ········· (18)

   Part One - Central Bank ········· (18)

      The Main Functions of the Central Bank ········· (18)

      Policy Instruments of Central Bank ········· (24)

   Part Two - Commercial Bank ········· (30)

      Personal Bank Services ········· (30)

      Types of Loans Granted by Commercial Banks ········· (36)

   Part Three - Regulation and Monetary Policies ········· (42)

      Monetary Policy ········· (42)

      Chinese Policy Makers will Boost Domestic Demand and Fight Inflation ········· (46)

Chapter Three: Investment System ········· (51)

   Part One - Investment Bank ········· (51)

      Investment Banks and Investment Bankers ········· (51)

　　　　Global Investment Banks Try China – Again ……………………（55）
　　Part Two – Investment Instruments ………………………………………（60）
　　　　China Sells More US T-Bonds ……………………………………（60）
　　　　Stocks and Stock Exchanges ………………………………………（64）
　　　　Restoring Faith in the Stock Market Essential to Economy …………（69）
　　　　Special Financial Instruments ……………………………………（73）
　　Part Three – Investment Risk Management ………………………………（78）
　　　　Who Is to Blame for the Subprime Crisis? ……………………（78）

Chapter Four: Insurance ……………………………………………（86）
　　Part One – Insurance ………………………………………………（86）
　　　　Filling China's Insurance Gaps ……………………………………（86）
　　Part Two – Life Insurance …………………………………………（91）
　　　　Secure Future for Life Insurance …………………………………（91）
　　Part Three – Non-life Insurance ……………………………………（96）
　　　　Property Insurance Provides Protection Against Risks to Property …（96）

Chapter Five: Financial Events ……………………………………（100）
　　The Asian Financial Crisis …………………………………………（100）
　　Why the Bundesbank Is Wrong ……………………………………（104）
　　Greed Is Not Good for Goldman ……………………………………（109）
　　A Possible Third Way for Bank Investors …………………………（114）

Chapter One: Financial Market and Money

Part One　Financial Market

Reading Comprehension

The Introduction to the Financial Market

A financial market is a market in which people and entities can trade financial securities, commodities, and other fungible items of value at low transaction costs and at prices that reflect supply and demand. Securities include stocks and bonds, and commodities include precious metals or agricultural goods.

There are both general markets (where many commodities are traded) and specialized markets (where only one commodity is traded). Markets work by placing many interested buyers and sellers, including households, firms, and government agencies, in one「place」, thus making it easier for them to find each other. An economy which relies primarily on interactions between buyers and sellers to allocate resources is known as a market economy in contrast either to a command economy or to a non-market economy such as a gift economy. In finance, financial markets facilitate:

- The raising of capital (in the capital markets)
- The transfer of risk (in the derivatives markets)
- Price discovery
- Global transactions with integration of financial markets
- The transfer of liquidity (in the money markets)
- International trade (in the currency markets)

and are used to match those who want capital to those who have it. Typically a borrower issues a receipt to the lender promising to pay back the capital. These receipts are securities which may be freely bought or sold. In return for lending money to the borrower, the lender will expect some compensation in the form of interest or dividends. This return on investment is a necessary part of markets to ensure that funds are supplied to them.

Within the financial sector, the term 「financial markets」 is often used to refer just to the markets that are used to raise finance: for long term finance, the 「capital markets」; for short term finance, the 「money markets」. Another common use of the term is as a catchall for all the markets in the financial sector, as per examples in the breakdown below.

- Capital markets which consist of:
  ▲ Stock markets, which provide financing through the issuance of shares or common stock, and enable the subsequent trading thereof.
  ▲ Bond markets, which provide financing through the issuance of bonds, and enable the subsequent trading thereof.
- Commodity markets, which facilitate the trading of commodities.
- Money markets, which provide short term debt financing and investment.
- Derivatives markets, which provide instruments for the management of financial risk.
- Futures markets, which provide standardized forward contracts for trading products at some future date; see also forward market.
- Insurance markets, which facilitate the redistribution of various risks.
- Foreign exchange markets, which facilitate the trading of foreign exchange.

The capital markets may also be divided into primary markets and secondary markets. Newly formed (issued) securities are bought or sold in primary markets, such as during initial public offerings. Secondary markets allow investors to buy and sell existing securities. The transactions in primary markets exist between issuers and investors, while in secondary markets transactions exist among investors.

Liquidity is a crucial aspect of securities that are traded in secondary markets. Liquidity refers to the ease with which a security can be sold without a loss of value. Securities with an active secondary market mean that there are many buyers and sellers at a given point in time. Investors benefit from liquid securities because they can sell their assets whenever they want; an illiquid security may force the seller to get rid of his assets at a large discount.

The financial market is broadly divided into 2 types: Capital Market and Money Market. The capital market is subdivided into Primary Market and Secondary Market.

New Words and Expressions

security	n.	證券
commodity	n.	商品
integration	n.	結合，整體
liquidity	n.	流動資產
money markets	n.	貨幣市場
derivatives markets	n.	衍生品市場
futures markets	n.	期貨市場
insurance markets	n.	保險市場
foreign exchange markets	n.	外匯市場
stock markets	n.	股票市場

Notes

1. Capital market: Capital markets are financial markets for the buying and selling of long-term debt- or equity-backed securities. These markets channel the wealth of savers to those who can put it to long-term productive use, such as companies or governments making long-term investments.

2. Money market: The money market became a component of the financial markets for assets involved in short-term borrowing, lending, buying and selling with original maturities of one year or less.

3. Derivatives market: The derivatives market is the financial market for derivatives, financial instruments like futures contracts or options, which are derived from other forms of assets. The market can be divided into two, that for exchange-traded derivatives and that for over-the-counter derivatives. The legal nature of these products is very different as well as the way they are traded, though many market participants are active in both.

4. Futures market: A futures exchange or futures market is a central financial exchange where people can trade standardized futures contracts; that is, a contract to buy

specific quantities of a commodity or financial instrument at a specified price with delivery set at a specified time in the future.

5. Foreign exchange market: The foreign exchange market (forex, FX, or currency market) is a form of exchange for the global decentralized trading of international currencies. Financial centers around the world function as anchors of trading between a wide range of different types of buyers and sellers around the clock, with the exception of weekends.

Exercises

I. Choose the best answer to the following questions.

1. What are the functions of the financial market?
    A. The raising of capital.
    B. The transfer of risk.
    C. International trade.
    D. All of the above.
2. What could be traded in the commodity market?
    A. Currency.
    B. Stocks.
    C. Bonds.
    D. Oil.

II. Translate the following sentences into Chinese.

1. A financial market is a market in which people and entities can trade financial securities, commodities, and other fungible items of value at low transaction costs and at prices that reflect supply and demand. Securities include stocks and bonds, and commodities include precious metals or agricultural goods.

2. The financial market is broadly divided into 2 types: Capital Market and Money Market. The capital market is subdivided into Primary Market and Secondary Market.

III. Read the text and answer the following questions.

1. What is a financial market?
2. What is the difference between the primary market and the secondary market when dealing with transactions?

A Short History of Modern Finance

The crash has been blamed on cheap money, Asian savings and greedy bankers. For many people, deregulation is the prime suspect.

The autumn of 2008 marks the end of an era. After a generation of standing ever further back from the business of finance, governments have been forced to step in to rescue banking systems and the markets. In America, the bulwark of free enterprise, and in Britain, the pioneer of privatization, financial firms have had to accept rescue and part-ownership by the state. As well as partial nationalisation, the price will doubtless be stricter regulation of the financial industry. To invert Karl Marx investment bankers may have nothing to gain but their chains.

The idea that the markets have ever been completely unregulated is a myth: just ask any firm that has to deal with the Securities and Exchange Commission (SEC) in America or its British equivalent, the Financial Services Authority (FSA). And cheap money and Asian savings also played a starring role in the credit boom. But the intellectual tide of the past 30 years has unquestionably been in favour of the primacy of markets and against regulation. Why was that so? Each step on the long deregulatory road seemed wise at the time and was usually the answer to some flaw in the system. The Anglo-Saxon economies may have led the way but continental Europe and Japan eventually followed (after a lot of grumbling) in their path.

It all began with floating currencies. In 1971 Richard Nixon sought to solve the mounting crisis of a large trade deficit and a costly war in Vietnam by suspending the dollar's convertibility into gold. In effect, that put an end to the Bretton Woods System of fixed exchange rates which had been created at the end of the second world war. Under Bretton Woods, capital could not flow freely from one country to another because of exchange controls. As one example, Britons heading abroad on their annual holidays in the late 1960s could take just £ 50 (then $120) with them. Investing abroad was expensive, so pension funds kept their money at home.

Once currencies could float, the world changed. Companies with costs in one currency and revenues in another needed to hedge exchange-rate risk. In 1972 a former lawyer named Leo Melamed was clever enough to see a business in this and launched currency futures on the Chicago Mercantile Exchange. Futures in commodities had existed for more than a century, enabling farmers to insure themselves against lower crop prices. But Mr Melamed saw that financial futures would one day be far larger than the commodities market. Today's complex derivatives are direct descendants of those early currency trades. Perhaps it was no coincidence that Chicago was also the centre of free-market economics. Led by Milton Friedman, its professors argued that Keynesian economics, with its emphasis on government intervention, had failed and that markets would be better at allocating capital than bureaucrats. After the economic turmoil of the 1970s, the Chicago school found a willing audience in Ronald Reagan and Margaret Thatcher, who were elected at the turn of the decade. The duo believed that freer markets would bring economic gains and that they would solidify popular support for the conservative cause. A nation of property-owners would be resistant to higher taxes and to left-wing attacks on business. Liberalized markets made it easier for homebuyers to get mortgages as credit controls were abandoned and more lenders entered the home-loan market.

Another consequence of a system of floating exchange rates was that capital controls were not strictly necessary. Continental European governments still feared the destabilising effect of hot money flows and created the European Monetary System in response. But Reagan and Mrs (now Lady) Thatcher took the plunge and abolished controls. The initial effects were mixed, with sharp appreciations of the dollar and pound causing problems for the two countries' exporters and exacerbating the recession of the early 1980s.

But the result was that institutions, such as insurance companies and pension funds, could move money across borders. In Britain that presented a challenge to the stockbrokers and marketmakers (known as jobbers) who had controlled share trading. Big investors complained that the brokers charged too much under an anti-competitive system of fixed commissions. At the same time, big international fund-managers found that the tiny jobbing firms had too little capital to handle their trades.

The Big Bang of 1986 abolished the distinction between brokers and jobbers and allowed foreign firms, with more capital, into the market. These firms could deal more cheaply and in greater size. New York had introduced a similar reform in 1975; in America's more developed domestic market, institutional investors had had the clout to demand the change long before their British counterparts.

These reforms had further consequences. By slashing commissions, they contributed to the long-term decline of broking as a source of revenue. The effect was disguised for a while by a higher volume of transactions. But the broker-dealers increasingly had to commit their own capital to deals. In turn, this made trading on their own account a potentially attractive source of revenue.

Over time, that changed the structure of the industry. Investment (or merchant) banks had traditionally been slim businesses, living off the wits of their employees and their ability to earn fees from advice. But the need for capital led them either to abandon their partnership structure and raise money on the stockmarket or to join up with commercial banks. In turn, that required the dilution and eventually, in 1999, the abolition of the old *Glass-Steagall Act*, devised in the Depression to separate American commercial and investment banking. Commercial banks were keen to move the other way. The plain business of corporate lending was highly competitive and retail banking required expensive branch networks. But strong balance-sheets gave commercial banks the chance to muscle investment banks out of the underwriting of securities. Investment banks responded by getting bigger.

Expansion and diversification took place against a remarkably favourable background. After the Federal Reserve, then chaired by Paul Volcker, broke the back of inflation in the early 1980s, asset prices (property, bonds, shares) rose for much of the next two decades. Trading in, or lending against, such assets was very profitable. And during the 「Great Moderation」recessions were short, limiting the damage done to banks' balance-sheets by bad debts.

New Words and Expressions

Securities and Exchange Commission	n.	美國證券交易委員會
Anglo-Saxon	n.	盎格魯—撒克遜
the Bretton Woods System	n.	布雷頓森林體系
hedge	v.	規避
Chicago Mercantile Exchange	n.	芝加哥商品交易市場
crop	n.	農作物
distinction	n.	區別
jobber	n.	批發商
slash	v.	消減

recession	n.	不景氣，衰退
reference	n.	提及；涉及；參考
affiliated	adj.	附屬的，有關聯的
distinguishing	adj.	有區別的

Notes

1. Securities and Exchange Commission (SEC): It is a federal agency in the United States. It holds primary responsibility for enforcing the federal securities laws and regulating the securities industry, the nation's stock and options exchanges, and other electronic securities markets in the United States.

2. Financial Services Authority (FSA): It is a quasi-judicial body responsible for the regulation of the financial services industry in the United Kingdom. Its board was appointed by the Treasury, although it operated independently of the government. It was structured as a company limited by guarantee and was funded entirely by fees charged to the financial services industry.

3. Keynesian Economics: It is the view that in the short run, especially during recessions, economic output is strongly influenced by aggregate demand (total spending in the economy). In the Keynesian view, aggregate demand does not necessarily equal the productive capacity of the economy; instead, it is influenced by a host of factors and sometimes behaves erratically, affecting production, employment, and inflation.

Exercises

I. Choose the best answer to the following questions.

1. What action did the U.S. government do in 1971?

    A. Put an end to the Bretton Woods System.

    B. Suspend the conversion between the dollar and gold.

    C. Suspend the Vietnam War.

    D. Trade the currency at the Chicago Mercantile Exchange.

2. Who did launch the currency futures on the Chicago Mercantile Exchange in 1972?

    A. Leo Melamed.

    B. President Reagan.

C. Lady Thatcher.

D. Karl Marx.

II. Translate the following passage into Chinese.

The autumn of 2008 marks the end of an era. After a generation of standing ever further back from the business of finance, governments have been forced to step in to rescue banking systems and the markets. In America, the bulwark of free enterprise, and in Britain, the pioneer of privatization, financial firms have had to accept rescue and part-ownership by the state. As well as partial nationalisation, the price will doubtless be stricter regulation of the financial industry.

III. Read the text and answer the following questions.

1. What happened after the currency became floating?

2. What are the effects of the floating currency to the economy?

Part Two   The Trend of the Financial Market

Reading Comprehension

Brokerage Firms Move to Set Up Futures Markets

Published April 4, 2013

Dow Jones Newswires

Some of the largest brokerages in the derivatives market are looking to start their own futures exchanges in response to new financial laws that could see business drain to established rival markets.

New York inter-dealer broker GFI Group Inc. (GFIG) submitted an application to open a proprietary U. S. futures exchange, according to the documents filed by the company, while rivals including Icap PLC and BGC Partners Inc. (BGCP) weighed similar efforts.

The moves come in response to new regulations outlined by the 2010 Dodd-Frank financial law, which tightened trading practices in the $639 trillion market for privately traded derivatives called swaps.

New regulations designed to curb systemic risks have added costs and complexity for the banks and asset managers that trade swaps, prompting some to evaluate futures contracts as a cheaper alternative for hedging risks.

That potential migration represents a threat to the franchises of inter-dealer brokers like GFI, which have for decades been the facilitators of swap trades among Wall Street banks.

GFI, which handles trading in energy, interest-rate and credit derivatives, aims to launch the GFI Futures Exchange LLC as a futures offering for customers that may otherwise take their business to a major exchange company such as CME Group Inc. (CME) or Intercontinental Exchange Inc. (ICE).

「The difference between the regulatory treatment of futures and swaps is unclear, and we want to be prepared to serve our clients' needs across all markets,」said a spokeswoman for GFI, in a statement.

GFI's effort comes as BGC, a rival inter-dealer broker based in New York, works to revamp ELX Futures LP, a market launched in 2009 as a competitor to CME in benchmark interest-rate contracts.

After failing to generate significant traction, BGC last year boosted its stake in the consortium-owned venture and is examining ways it can serve a different purpose under the Dodd-Frank regime, according to executives. Representatives for BGC did not immediately respond to requests for comment.

London-based Icap, the world's largest broker of trades between banks, acquired PLUS Stock Exchange PLC last May, rebranding it as ISDX and planning to list futures on the platform.

「At the time that ISDX was rebranded, we indicated that we didn't have a definitive timeline as to when we might start considering launching any listed derivatives or futures, but it is something we are investigating,」said Chris Ferreri, managing director of hybrid brokering at ICAP U.S.

Futures are openly traded on exchanges or「designated contract markets」, while swaps are negotiated privately been two counterparties and traded off exchange. As a result of the 2010 Dodd Frank financial overhaul law, however, most swaps will have to be traded on open platforms for the first time and centrally processed by clearinghouses, much like futures.

However, rules have yet to be finalized for so-called swap execution facilities, the venues on which many swaps will have to be traded, and in the meantime futures exchanges like ICE and CME are pushing ahead with new contracts meant to replicate swaps.

New Words and Expressions

brokerage	n. 代理人
submit	v. 提交
rival	n. 對手
regulation	n. 規則
derivatives	n. 衍生品
swaps	n. 掉期
curb	v. 控制，限制
systemic	adj. 系統的，全局的
hedge	v. 迴避，多頭下注以避免損失
clearinghouse	n. 票據交換所

Notes

1. SWAPS: a swap is a derivative in which counterparties exchange cash flows of one party's financial instrument for those of the other party's financial instrument. The benefits in question depend on the type of financial instruments involved.

2. Derivative: it is a term that refers to a wide variety of financial instruments or contracts whose value is derived from the performance of underlying market factors, such as market securities or indices, interest rates, currency exchange rates, and commodity, credit, and equity prices.

3. Brokerage: it is a financial institution that facilitates the buying and selling of financial securities between a buyer and a seller. Brokerage firms serve a clientele of investors who trade public stocks and other securities, usually through the firm's agent stockbrokers.

4. CME Group Inc: it is the world's largest futures exchange company. It owns and operates large derivatives and futures exchanges in Chicago and New York City, as well as online trading platforms. It also owns the Dow Jones stock and financial indexes, and CME Clearing Services, which provides settlement and clearing of exchange trades.

5. Clearinghouse: it is a financial institution that provides clearing and settlement services for financial and commodities derivatives and securities transactions. These transactions may be executed on a futures exchange or securities exchange, as well as off-exchange in the over-the-counter (OTC) market.

Exercises

I. Choose the best answer to the following question.

Why did the large brokerage start their own futures exchange?

    A. To earn more money.

    B. To response to new regulations.

    C. To outperform the rivals.

    D. To play monopoly in the market.

II. Translate the following sentences into Chinese.

1. 「The difference between the regulatory treatment of futures and swaps is unclear, and we want to be prepared to serve our clients' needs across all markets,」said a spokeswoman for GFI, in a statement.

2. Futures are openly traded on exchanges or 「designated contract markets」, while swaps are negotiated privately been two counterparties and traded off exchange. As a result of the 2010 Dodd Frank financial overhaul law, however, most swaps will have to be traded on open platforms for the first time and centrally processed by clearinghouses, much like futures.

III. Discuss the following question.

Why has China reformed...?

Part Three   Money

A currency (from Middle English *curraunt*, meaning in circulation) in the most specific use of the word refers to money in any form when in actual use or circulation, as a medium of exchange, especially circulating paper money. This use is synonymous with banknotes, or (sometimes) with banknotes plus coins, meaning the physical tokens used for money by a government.

A much more general use of the word currency is anything that is used in any circumstances, as a medium of exchange. In this use, 「currency」 is a synonym for the concept of money.

A definition of intermediate generality is that a currency is a system of money (monetary units) in common use, especially in a nation. Under this definition, British pounds, U.S. dollars, and European euros are different types of currency, or currencies. Currencies in this definition need not be physical objects, but as stores of value are subject to trading between nations in foreign exchange markets, which determine the relative values of the different currencies. Currencies in the sense used by foreign exchange markets, are defined by governments, and each type has limited boundaries of acceptance.

1. The History of Money

- Early Currency

Currency evolved from two basic innovations, both of which had occurred by 2000 BC. Originally money was a form of receipt, representing grain stored in temple granaries in Sumer in ancient Mesopotamia, then Ancient Egypt.

This first stage of currency, where metals were used to represent stored value, and symbols to represent commodities, formed the basis of trade in the Fertile Crescent for over 1,500 years. However, the collapse of the Near Eastern trading system pointed to a flaw: in an era where there was no place that was safe to store value, the value of a circulating medium could only be as sound as the forces that defended that store. Trade could only reach as far as the credibility of that military. By the late Bronze Age, however, a series of treaties had established safe passage for merchants around the Eastern Mediterranean, spreading from Minoan Crete and Mycenae in the northwest to Elam and Bahrain in the southeast. Although it is not known what functioned as a currency to facilitate these exchanges, it is thought that ox-hide shaped ingots of copper, produced in Cyprus may have functioned as a currency. It is thought that the increase in piracy and raiding associated with the Bronze Age collapse, possibly produced by the Peoples of the Sea, brought this trading system to an end. It was only with the recovery of Phoenician trade in the ninth and tenth centuries BC that saw a return to prosperity, and the appearance of real coinage, possibly first in Anatolia with Croesus of Lydia and subsequently with the Greeks and Persians. In Africa many forms of value store have been used including beads, ingots, ivory, various forms of weapons, livestock, the manilla currency, ochre and other earth oxides, and so on. The manilla rings of West Africa were one of the currencies used from the 15th century onwards to buy and sell slaves. African currency is still notable for its variety, and in many places various forms of barter still apply.

- Modern Currencies

Currency use is based on the concept of lex monetae that a sovereign state decides which currency it shall use. Currently, the International Organization for Standardization has introduced a three-letter system of codes (ISO 4217) to define currency (as opposed to simple names or currency signs), in order to remove the confusion that there are dozens of currencies called the dollar and many called the franc. Even the pound is used in nearly a dozen different countries, all, of course, with wildly differing values. In general, the three-letter code uses the ISO 3166-1 country code for the first two letters and the first letter of the name of the currency (D for dollar, for instance) as the third letter. United States currency, for instance is globally referred to as USD. It is also possible for a currency to be internet-based and digital, for instance, Bitcoin, the Ripple Pay system or MintChip, and not tied to any specific country. The International Monetary Fund uses a variant system when referring to national currencies.

2. Regulation by Central Bank

In most cases, a central bank has monopoly control over emission of coins and banknotes (fiat money) for its own area of circulation (a country or group of countries); it regulates the production of currency by banks (credit) through monetary policy.

In order to facilitate trade between these currency zones, there are different exchange rates, which are the prices at which currencies (and the goods and services of individual currency zones) can be exchanged against each other. Currencies can be classified as either floating currencies or fixed currencies based on their exchange rate regime.

In cases where a country does have control of its own currency, that control is exercised either by a central bank or by the Ministry of Finance. In either case, the institution that has control of monetary policy is referred to as the monetary authority. Monetary authorities have varying degrees of autonomy from the governments that create them. In the United States, the Federal Reserve System operates without direct oversight by the legislative or executive branches. A monetary authority is created and supported by its sponsoring government, so independence can be reduced by the legislative or executive authority that creates it.

Several countries can use the same name for their own distinct currencies (for example, dollar in Australia, Canada and the United States). By contrast, several countries can also use the same currency (for example, the euro), or one country can declare the currency of another country to be legal tender. For example, Panama and El Salvador have declared U. S. currency to be legal tender, and from 1791 – 1857, Spanish silver coins were legal tender in the United States. At various times countries have either re-stamped foreign coins, or used currency board issuing one note of currency for each note of a foreign government held, as Ecuador currently does.

Each currency typically has a main currency unit (the dollar, for example, or the euro) and a fractional currency, often valued at 1/100 of the main currency: 100 cents = 1 dollar, 100 centimes = 1 franc, 100 pence = 1 pound, although units of 1/10 or 1/1,000 are also common. Some currencies do not have any smaller units at all, such as the Icelandic króna.

Mauritania and Madagascar are the only remaining countries that do not use the decimal system; instead, the Mauritanian ouguiya is divided into 5 khoums, while the Malagasy ariary is divided into 5 iraimbilanja. In these countries, words like dollar or pound「were simply names for given weights of gold」.

New Words and Expressions

currency	n.	貨幣
banknote	n.	鈔票
ancient	adj.	古代的
Egypt	n.	埃及
innovation	n.	發明，創造
fertile	adj.	肥沃的
military	adj.	軍隊的
credibility	n.	可信度
Mediterranean	n.	地中海，地中海沿岸諸國
treaty	n.	條約
livestock	n.	家畜
Greek	adj.	希臘的

Persian	*adj.*	波斯的
barter	*v.*	進行物物交換
Franc	*n.*	法郎
Pound	*n.*	英鎊
monopoly	*n.*	壟斷
regime	*n.*	政權，體制

Notes

1. Currency: in the most specific use, the word refers to money in any form when in actual use or circulation, as a medium of exchange, especially circulating paper money.

2. Fertile Crescent: it is a crescent-shaped region containing the comparatively moist and fertile land of otherwise arid and semi-arid Western Asia, and the Nile Valley and Nile Delta of northeast Africa.

3. Banknote: it is commonly known as a bill in the United States and Canada. It is a type of currency, and is commonly used as legal tender in many jurisdictions.

4. Monetary policy: it is the process by which the monetary authority of a country controls the supply of money, often targeting a rate of interest for the purpose of promoting economic growth and stability.

Exercises

I. Choose the best answer to the following questions.

1. When did the first stage of currency start?
    A. 2000 BC.
    B. 1,000 years ago.
    C. Bronze Age.
    D. Modern Age.

2. During the first stage, what was the currency used for?
    A. To represent grain value stored.
    B. To buy and sell slaves.
    C. To exchange with other currencies.
    D. To pay for food.

3. In a country, the control of the currency could be exercised by_____.

   A. a central bank

   B. the president

   C. the congress

   D. the IMF

II. Translate the following sentences into Chinese.

1. In the United States, the Federal Reserve System operates without direct oversight by the legislative or executive branches. A monetary authority is created and supported by its sponsoring government, so independence can be reduced by the legislative or executive authority that creates it.

2. Currency evolved from two basic innovations, both of which had occurred by 2000 BC. Originally money was a form of receipt, representing grain stored in temple granaries in Sumer in ancient Mesopotamia, then Ancient Egypt.

III. Read the text and answer the following questions.

1. Which countries can use the same name for their own distinct currencies?

2. Which department has the right to control of its own currency in the country?

金融英語閱讀 Financial English Reading

Chapter Two: Banking System

Part One　Central Bank

Reading Comprehension

The Main Functions of the Central Bank

A central bank, reserve bank, or monetary authority is the entity responsible for the monetary policy of a country or of a group of member states. It is a bank that can lend to other banks in times of need. Its primary responsibility is to maintain the stability of the national currency and money supply, but more active duties include controlling subsidized-loan interest rates, and acting as a lender of last resort to the banking sector during times of financial crisis (private banks often being integral to the national financial system). It may also have supervisory powers, to ensure that banks and other financial institutions do not behave recklessly or fraudulently. Most rich countries today have an 「independent」 central bank, that is, one which operates under rules designed to prevent political interference. Examples include the European Central Bank (ECB) and the Federal Reserve System in the United States. Some central banks are publicly owned, and others are privately. For example, the Reserve Bank of India is publicly owned and directly governed by the Indian government. Another example is the United States Federal Reserve, which is a privately owned, for-profit corporation. The major difference is that government-owned central banks do not charge the taxpayers interest on the national currency, whereas privately owned central banks do charge interest.

In Europe prior to the 17th century most money was commodity money, typically gold or silver. However, promises to pay were widely circulated and accepted as value at least five hundred years earlier in both Europe and Asia. The medieval European Knights Templar ran probably the best known early prototype of a central banking system, as their promises to pay were widely regarded, and many regard their activities as having laid the basis for the modern banking system. At about the same time, Kublai Khan of the Mongols introduced fiat currency to China, which was imposed by force by the confiscation of specie. The oldest central bank in the world is the Riksbank in Sweden, which was opened in 1668 with help from Dutch businessmen. This was followed in 1694 by the Bank of England, created by Scottish businessman William Paterson in the City of London at the request of the English government to help for a war. The US Federal Reserve was created by the U. S. Congress through the passing of the Glass-Owen Bill, signed by President Woodrow Wilson on December 23, 1913.

The People's Bank of China evolved its role as a central bank starting in about 1983 with the introduction of market reforms in that country. By 2000 the People's Bank of China was in all senses a modern central bank, and emerged as such partly in response to the European Central bank. This is the most modern bank model and was introduced with the euro to coordinate the European national banks which continue to separately manage their respective economies other than currency exchange and base interest rates. Functions of a central bank (not all functions are carried out by all banks):

- implementing monetary policy
- controlling the nation's entire money supply
- acting as the government's banker and banker's bank (⌈lender of last resort⌋)
- managing the country's foreign exchange and gold reserves and Government's stock register
- regulating and supervising the banking industry
- setting the official interest rate – used to manage both inflation and the country's exchange rate – and ensuring that this rate takes effect via a variety of policy mechanisms

Monetary Policy

Central banks implement a country's chosen monetary policy. At the most level, this involves establishing what form of currency the country may have, whether a fiat currency, gold-backed currency (disallowed for countries with membership of the

IMF), currency board or a currency union. When a country has its own national currency, this involves the issue of some form of standard currency, which is essentially a form of promissory note: a promise to exchange the note for 「money」 under certain circumstances. Historically, this was a promise to exchange the money for precious metals in some fixed amount. When many currencies are fiat money, the 「promise to pay」 consists of more than a promise to pay the same sum in the same currency.

In many countries, the central bank may use another country's currency directly (in a currency union), or indirectly (by using a currency board). In the latter case, local currency is backed by the central bank's holding foreign currency in a fixed-ratio; this mechanism is used, notably, in Bulgaria.

In the countries with fiat money, monetary policy may be used as a slow form for the interest rate targets and other active measures undertaken by the monetary authority.

Currency Issuance

Many central banks are 「banks」 in the sense that they hold assets (foreign exchange, gold, and other financial assets) and liabilities. A central bank's primary liabilities are the currency outstanding, and these liabilities are backed by the assets the bank owns.

Central banks generally earn money by issuing currency notes and 「selling」 them to the public for interest-bearing assets, such as government bonds. Since currency usually pays no interest, the difference in interest generates income called seigniorage. In most central banking systems, this income is remitted to the government. The European Central Bank remits its interest income to its owners, the central banks of the member countries of the European Union.

Although central banks generally hold government debt, in some countries the outstanding amount of government debt is smaller than the amount the central bank may wish to hold. In many countries, central banks may hold significant amounts of foreign currency assets, rather than assets in their own national currency, particularly when the national currency is fixed to other currencies.

Naming of Central Banks

There is no standard terminology for the name of a central bank, but many countries use the 「Bank of Country」 form (e.g., Bank of England, Bank of Canada, Bank of Russia). Some are styled 「national」 banks, such as the National Bank of Ukraine; but the term 「national bank」 is more often used by privately-owned commercial banks, especially in the United States. In other cases, central banks may incorporate the word 「Central」 (e. g. , European Central Bank, Central Bank of Ireland). The word 「Reserve」 is also often included, such as the Reserve Bank of Australia, and U. S. Federal Reserve System. Many countries have state-owned banks or other quasi-government entities that have entirely separate functions, such as financing imports and exports.

In some countries, the term national bank may be used to indicate both the monetary authority and the leading banking entity, such as the USS's Gosbank (state bank). In other countries, the term national bank may be used to indicate that the central bank's goals are broader than monetary stability, such as full employment, industrial development, or other goals.

Interest Rate Interventions

Typically a central bank controls certain types of short-term interest rates. These influence the stock and bond markets as well as mortgage and other interest rates. The European Central Bank for example announces its interest rate at the meeting of Governing Council; in the case of the Federal Reserve, the Board of Governors.

Both the Federal Reserve and ECB are composed of one or more central bodies that are responsible for the main decisions about interest rates and type of open market operations, and several branches to execute its policies. In the case of the Fed, they are the local Federal Reserve Banks; for the ECB they are the national central banks.

Limits of Enforcement Power

Contrary to popular perception, central banks are not all-powerful and have limited powers to put their policies into effect. Most importantly, although the perception by the public may be that the 「central bank」 controls some or all interest rates and currency rates, economic theory (and substantial empirical evidence) shows that it is impossible to do both at once in an open economy. Robert Mundell's 「impossible trinity」 is the most famous formulation of these limited powers, and postulates that it is impossible to target monetary policy (broadly, interest rates), the exchange rate (through a fixed rate) and maintain free capital movement. Since most Western economies are now considered 「open」 with free capital movement, this essentially means that central banks may target interest rates or exchange rates with credibility, but not both at once.

Even when targeting interest rates, most central banks have limited ability to influence the rates actually paid by private individuals and companies. In the most famous case of policy failure, George Soros arbitraged the pound sterling's relationship to the ECU and (after making $2 billion himself and forcing the UK to spend over $8 billion defending the pound) forced it to abandon its policy. Since then he has been a harsh critic of clumsy bank policies and argued that no one should be able to do what he did.

The most complex relationships are those between the yuan and the US dollar, and between the euro and its neighbours. The situation in Cuba is exceptional as to require the Cuban peso to be dealt with simply as an exception, since the United States forbids direct trade with Cuba. US dollars were ubiquitous in Cuba's economy after its legalization in 1991, but were officially removed from circulation in 2004 and replaced by the convertible peso.

New Words and Expressions

intervention	n.	干涉
Fiat currency	n.	法定貨幣
IMF	n.	國際貨幣基金組織
monetary	adj.	貨幣的
European	adj.	歐洲的
independent	adj.	獨立的
Federal Reserve System	n.	聯邦儲備制度
circulate	v.	循環
Sweden	n.	瑞典
implement	v.	實現，執行
promise	v.	承諾
enforcement	n.	強制，執行
convertible	adj.	可轉換的

Notes

1. Monetary policy: it involves establishing what form of currency the country may use, whether a fiat currency, gold-backed currency, currency board or a currency union.

2. Central bank: a financial institution designated by the central government to formulate and implement monetary policy and to supervise and regulate the financial industry.

3. Regulating: as a regulator, the central bank formulates rules that govern the conduct of financial institutions.

4. Supervising: as a supervisor, the central bank examines and monitors institutions to help ensure that they operate in a safe and sound manner and comply with the laws and rules that apply to them.

Exercises

I. Choose the best answer to the following questions.

1. What is the main function of a central bank?
    A. Naming the central bank.
    B. Implementing monetary policy.
    C. Providing depository services.
    D. Charging interest rate.

2. What terminology is used to name the central bank?
    A. no standard terminology
    B. 「bank of country」
    C. 「reserve」
    D. 「national bank」

3. When did the People's Bank of China become the central bank of China?
    A. 1978　　　　　　　　　　B. 1983
    C. 1949　　　　　　　　　　D. 1990

II. Translate the following sentences into Chinese.

1. The main functions of a central bank are implementing monetary policy, controlling the nation's entire money supply, acting as the government's banker and the bankers' bank, managing the country's foreign exchange and gold reserves and the government's stock register, regulating and supervising the banking industry, setting the official interest rate – used to manage both inflation and the country's exchange rate – and ensuring that this rate takes effect via a variety of policy mechanisms.

2. A central bank's primary liabilities are the currency outstanding, and these lia-

bilities are backed by the assets the bank owns.

III. Read the text and answer the following questions.
1. How do central banks earn money?
2. What is primary responsibility of the central bank?

Policy Instruments of the Central Bank

The main monetary policy instruments available to central banks are open market operation, bank reserve requirement, interest rate policy, relending and rediscount (including using the term repurchase market), and credit policy (often coordinated with trade policy). While capital adequacy is important, it is defined and regulated by the Bank for International Settlements, and central banks in practice generally do not apply stricter rules.

To enable open market operations, a central bank must hold foreign exchange reserve (usually in the form of government bonds) and official gold reserves. It will often have some influence over any official or mandated exchange rates: some exchange rates are managed, some are market based (free float) and many are somewhere in between (「managed float」 or 「dirty float」).

Interest Rates

By far the most visible and obvious power of many modern central banks is to influence market interest rates; contrary to popular belief they rarely 「set」 rates to a number. Although the mechanism differs from country to country, most use similar mechanism based on a central bank's ability to create as much fiat money as required.

The mechanism to move the market towards a 「target rate」 (whichever specific rate is used) is generally to lend money or borrow money in theoretically unlimited quantities, until the targeted market rate is sufficiently close to the target. Central banks may do so by lending money to and borrowing money from (taking deposits form) a limited number of qualified banks, or by purchasing and selling bonds. As an example of this function, the Bank of Canada sets a target overnight rate, and a band of plus or minus 0.25%. Qualified banks borrow from each other within this band, but never above or below, because the central bank will always lend to them at the top of the band, and take deposits at the bottom of the band; in principle, the capacity to borrow and lend at the extremes of the band are unlimited. Other central banks use similar mechanism. It is also notable that the target rates are generally short-term rates. The actual rate that borrowers and lenders receive on the market will depend on (perceived) credit risk, maturity and other factors. For example, a central bank might set a target rate for overnight lending of 4.5%, but rates for (equivalent risk) five-year bonds might be 5%, 4.75%, or, in cases of inverted yield curves, even below the short-term rate. Many central banks have one primary 「headline」 rate that is quoted as the 「central bank rate」. In practice, they will have other tools and rates that are used, but only one that is rigorously targeted and enforced. 「The rate at which the central bank lends money can indeed be chosen at will by the central bank; this is the rate that makes the financial headlines.」 – Henry C. K. Liu. Liu explains further that 「the U.S. central-bank lending rate is known as the Fed funds rate. The Fed sets a target for the Fed funds rate, which its Open Market Committee tries to match by lending or borrowing in the money market – a fiat money system set by command of the central bank. The Fed is the head of the central bank because the U.S. dollar is the key reserve currency for international trade. The global money market is a USA dollar market. All other currencies markets revolve around the U.S. dollar market.」 Accordingly the situation is not typical of central banks in general. A typical central bank has several interest rates or monetary policy tools it can set to influence markets.

- Marginal lending rate (currently 4.25% in the Eurozone): a fixed rate institution to borrow money from the central bank. (In the USA this is the discount rate)
- Main refinancing rate (3.75% in the Eurozone): the publicly visible interest rate the central bank announces. It is also known as *minimum bid rate* serving as a bidding floor for refinancing loans. (In the USA this is called federal funds rate)
- Deposit rate (3.25% in the Eurozone): the rate parties receive for the deposit at the central bank.

These directly affect the rates in the money market, the market for short-term loans.

Open Market Operations

Through open market operations, a central bank influences the money supply in economy directly. Each time it buys securities, exchanging money for security, it raises the money supply. Conversely, selling of securities lowers money supply. Buying of securities thus amounts to printing new money while lowering supply of the specific security. The main open market operations are:

- Temporary lending of money for collateral securities (「Reverse Operations」or 「Repurchase Operations」, otherwise known as the 「repo」market). These operations are carried out on a regular basis, where fixed maturity loans (of 1 week and 1 month for the ECB) are auctioned off.
- Buying or selling securities (「direct operations」) on ad-hoc basis.
- Foreign exchange operations such as forex swaps.

All of these interventions can also influence the foreign exchange market and thus the exchange rate. For example, the People's Bank of China and the Bank of Japan have on occasion bought several hundred billions of U.S. Treasuries, presumably in order to stop the decline of the U.S. dollar versus the Renminbi and the yen.

Capital Requirements

All banks are required to hold a certain percentage of their assets as capital, a rate which may be established by the central bank or the banking supervisor. For international banks, including the 55 member central banks of the Bank for International Settlements, the threshold is 8% (see the Basel Capital Accords) of risk-adjusted assets, whereby certain assets (such as government bonds) are considered t have lower risk and are either partially or fully excluded from total assets for the purpose of calculating capital adequacy. Partly due to concerns about asset inflation and repurchase agreements, capital requirements may be considered more effective than deposit/reserve requirements in preventing indefinite lending: when at the threshold, a bank cannot extend another loan without acquiring further capital on its balance sheet.

Reserve Requirements

Another significant power that central banks hold is the ability to establish reserve requirements for other banks. By requiring that a percentage of liabilities be held as cash or deposited with the central bank (or other agency), limits are set on the money supply.

In practice, many banks are required to hold a percentage of their deposits as reverses; such legal reserve requirements were introduced in the nineteenth century to reduce the risk of banks overextending themselves and suffering form bank runs, as this could lead to knock-on effects on other banks. As the early 20th century gold standard and late 20th century dollar hegemony evolved, and as banks proliferated and engaged in more complex transactions and were able to profit from dealings globally on a moment's notice, these practices became mandatory, if only to ensure that there was some limit on the ballooning of money supply. Such limits have become harder to enforce. The People's Bank of China retains (and uses) more powers over reserve because yuan that it manages is a non-convertible currency.

Even if reserve were not a legal requirement, prudence would ensure that banks would hold a certain percentage of their assets in the form of cash reserves. It is common to think of commercial banks as passive receivers of deposits from their customers and, for many purposes, this is still an accurate view.

This passive view of bank activity is misleading when it comes to considering what determines the nation's money supply and credit. Loan activity by banks plays a fundamental role in determining the money supply. The money deposited by commercial banks at the central bank is the real money in the banking system; other versions of what is commonly thought of as money are merely promises to pay real money. These promises to pay are circulatory multiples of real money. For general purposes, people perceive money as the amount shown in financial transactions or amount shown in their bank accounts. But bank accounts record both credit and debits that cancel each other, only the remaining central-bank money after aggregate settlement − final money − can take only one of two forms:
- Physical cash, which is rarely used in wholesale financial markets.
- Central-bank money.

The currency component of the money supply is far smaller than the deposit component. Currency and bank reserves together make up the monetary base, called M1 and M2.

Exchange Requirements

To influence the money supply, some central banks may require that some or all foreign exchange receipts (generally from exports) be exchanged for the local currency. The rate that is used to purchase local currency may be market-based or arbitrarily set by the bank. This tool is generally used in the countries with non-convertible currencies or partially-convertible currencies. The recipient of the local currency may be allowed to freely dispose of the funds, required to hold the funds with the central bank for some period of time, or allowed to use the funds subject to certain restrictions. In other cases, the ability to hold or use the foreign exchange may be otherwise limited.

In this method, money supply is increased by the central bank when it purchases the foreign currency by issuing (selling) the local currency. The central bank may subsequently reduce the money supply by various means, including selling bonds or foreign exchange interventions.

Margin Requirements and Other Tools

In some countries central banks may have other tools that work indirectly to limit lending practices and otherwise restrict or regulate capital markets. Fox example, a central bank may regulate margin lending, whereby individuals or companies may borrow against pledged securities. The margin requirement establishes a minimum ratio of the value of the securities to the amount borrowed.

Central banks often have requirements for the quality of assets that may be held by financial institutions; these requirements may act as a limit on the amount of risk and leverage created by the financial system. These requirements may be direct, such as requiring certain assets to bear certain minimum credit ratings, or indirect, by the central bank lending to counterparties only when security of a certain quality is pledged as collateral.

Examples of Use

The People's Bank of China has been forced into particularly aggressive and differentiating tactics by the extreme complexity and rapid expansion of the economy it manages. It imposed some absolute restrictions on lending to specific industries in 2003, and continues to require 1% and 3% more reserves from large urban banks (typically focusing on export) than rural ones. This is not by any means an unusual situation. The USA historically had very wide ranges of reserve requirements between its dozen branches. Domestic development is thought to be optimized mostly by reserve requirements rather than by capital adequacy methods, since they can be more finely tuned and regionally varied.

New Words and Expressions

crunch	*n.*	緊縮
specie	*n.*	硬幣
credit crunch		信貸緊縮

currency outstanding		貨幣流通
seigniorage	n.	鑄幣稅
ad-hoc basis		專責性質
collateral	n.	抵押品，擔保品

Notes

1. Equity financing: the act of raising money for company activities by selling common or preferred stock to individuals or institutional investors. In return for the money paid, shareholders receive ownership interests in the corporation.

2. Open market operations: Open market operations are the means of implementing monetary policy by which a central bank controls its national money supply by buying and selling government securities, or other financial instruments. Monetary targets, such as interest rates or exchange rates, are used to guide this implementation.

3. Commodity money: Commodity money is money whose value comes from a commodity out of which it is made. It is objects that have value in themselves as well as for use as money. Examples of commodities that have been used as mediums of exchange include gold, silver, copper, salt, peppercorns, large stones, decorated belts, shells, cigarettes, cannabis, candy, barley, etc. These items were sometimes used in a metric of perceived value in conjunction to one another, in various commodity valuation or price system economies.

4. The Basel Accord(s): The Basel Accord(s) or Basel Accord(s) refers to the banking supervision accords (recommendations on banking laws and regulations). Basel I and II were issued by Basel Committee on Banking Supervision (BCBS).

5. Lender of last resort: A lender of last resort is an institution willing to credit when no one else will.

6. Margin lending: In finance, a margin is collateral that the holder of a position in securities, options, or futures contracts has to deposit to cover the credit risk of his counterparty (most often his broker).

Exercises

I. Choose the best answer to the following questions.

1. What is the current marginal lending rate in the Euro-zone?

A. 4.25%   B. 3.75%

C. 3.25%   D. 4.75%

2. What is the capital requirement?

   A. All banks are required to hold a certain percentage of their assets as capital.

   B. All banks are required to hold a certain percentage of their liabilities as cash.

   C. All banks are required to hold a certain percentage of their liabilities as depository.

   D. None of the above.

II. Translate the following sentences into Chinese.

1. All banks are required to hold a certain percentage of their assets as capital, a rate which may be established by the central bank or the banking supervisor.

2. In practice, many banks are required to hold a percentage of their deposits as reserves, such legal reserve requirements were introduced in the nineteenth century reduce the risk of banks overextending themselves and suffering form bank runs, as this could lead to knock - on effects on other banks.

III. Read the text and answer the following questions.

1. What are the functions of legal reserve requirements?

2. Why do central banks establish reserve requirements for other banks?

Part Two Commercial Bank

Reading Comprehension

Personal Bank Services

Checking Account

A checking account is a service provided by financial institutions (banks, savings and loans, credit unions, etc.) which allows individuals and businesses to deposit money and withdraw funds from a federally-protected account. The terms of a checking account may vary from bank to bank, but in general a checking account holder can use personal checks in place of cash to pay debts. He or she can also use electronic debit cards or ATM cards to access individual accounts or make cash withdrawals.

Virtually every bank offers some form of checking account service for their customers. Some may require a minimal initial deposit before establishing a new account, alongwith proof of identification and address. A student or other low-income applicant may opt for a no-frills checking account which does not charge fees for the use of personal checks and other services. Others may benefit from interest payments by maintaining a high minimum balance each month. Some states are required by law to provide a 「lifeline」checking account option for senior citizens and low-income customers. This type of checking account waives many of the fees banks may charge, such as monthly service fees for low balances and surcharges for ATM usage.

A typical checking account is handled through careful posting of deposits and withdrawals. The account holder has a supply of official checks which contain all of the essential routing and mailing information. When a check is filled out currently, the recipient treats it the same as cash and completes the transaction. After this check has been deposited into the recipient's own bank account, a bank worker files the check electronically and the check writer's bank receives the cancelled check and amount to be debited (withdrawn) from the check writer's account. This process continues for every check written against an individual checking account.

Owners of a checking account are ultimately responsible for keeping track of their available funds, even though the bank will routinely issue its own accounting statements. Checks must represent an actual amount of money contained in the checking account itself. If a check is written for an amount higher than the available balance, the check writer faces numerous fees and possible legal action. The recipient of the bad check can demand immediate cash payment for the original debt as well as a substantial fee for the returned check. Some banks will protect checking account holders by making the proper payments and notifying the check writer that an overdraft has taken place. Most often the bank will recoup their losses through substantial service charges, so it pays to avoid writing checks when the balance is unknown.

Most banks have several different methods which allow checking account customers to check their balances and reconcile their records. Printed monthly statements of debits and credits (deposits) are mailed to individual account holders. ATM machines offer an option to check the current balance, while online or phone-in accounts can provide real time updates on which checks have been processed and which are still outstanding. This information can be compared with the entries recorded in a journal called a check register.

As long as the account holder maintains accurate financial records, a checking account provides a safe and efficient way to pay bills and deposit money from payroll checks and other income sources. A saving account may pay more interest over time, but a checking account replaces the need for large amounts of cash to satisfy routine debts such as rent or mortgage payments, credit card bills and utility bills.

Savings Account

A savings account typically refers to an account in which one places money to earn a small amount of interest. The savings account funds are usually easily accessible, though some banks do charge for withdrawing money early. In most cases, people can withdraw money from a savings account at any time, at least at any time the bank is open, or one has access to the bank's ATM.

The term 「bank」 is used here loosely. Not only banks, but also credit unions, and money market fund companies can offer a savings account to customers. In addition to earning interest on your deposits, the savings account also provides a safe place to put your money, far better than stowing it in the mattress or the cookie jar. If the bank declares bankruptcy is the target of embezzlement, or mismanages its funds, the Federal Deposit Insurance Corporation (FDIC) insures your account, up to $100,000 US dollars (USD). In fact, a requirement when shopping for a savings account is to look for one that is FDIC-insured. If your savings account isn't FDIC-insured, you might have difficulty if the bank encounters financial problems. Most banks, credit unions and money market funds do offer this insurance.

You also need to shop around for a savings account that offers the best interest rates. In the past, it was often the case that banks offered a slightly higher interest rate than did credit unions. This is because credit unions attempt to confer lower interest rates than banks to their customers borrowing money. Now sometimes credit unions are quite competitive in rates. Money market funds tend to be the most changeable in rates. Interest earned will depend upon the stock market, so they can be very high at some times and low at others.

Many people wonder how a saving account works and is profitable to the bank or other financial institutions. The simple explanation is that you are actually lending your money to the financial institution. In return for this loan, the bank offers you part of the interest they charge customers. Thus the bank makes a profit and you make a profit on any money in a savings account.

Sometimes people might use an interest checking account instead of a savings account. If you really plan not to spend your money for a few months, it makes sense to use a savings account instead. An interest checking account pays much less interest than does a savings account, and normally requires maintaining a high minimum balance, about $1,000 USD. If this balance is not maintained, the checking account may actually charge you bank fees for your use of the account, which nullifies any potential interest earned.

Most savings accounts require a minimum deposit, usually $100 USD. An exception exists for children, who often have a savings account as their first bank account. Banks are very accommodating to the children who wish to open a savings account because it is a way to build its future base of customers. Usually kids can open a savings account with about $5 USD.

The high competition for your temporary loan to banks means you should shop around prior to choosing a savings account. Some companies will offer terrific incentives. In 2007 Ameritrade began offering a money market savings account, which if kept open for a year would pay a $100 USD bonus at the end of the first year. Money expert Suze Orman, who normally doesn't endorse specific products, touted this as one of the best offers available to people who want to save their money.

A Certificate of Deposit

A certificate of deposit, also called a CD, is a type of savings certificate. A client deposits a certain amount of funds with a bank for a fixed period, usually from one to five years although longer terms are possible, and in return is guaranteed a locked interest rate which is higher than that of a traditional savings account. For people who want non-risky methods of investment with guaranteed returns, such as the elderly, the youth wanting to set money aside, or people with limited funds, a certificate of deposit is an excellent investment alternative, because when the certificate of deposit is held by the Federal Deposit Insurance Corporation (FDIC) insured bank and is for less than $100,000 USD, the client will never lose his or her money.

A certificate of deposit can take a wide variety of forms which are negotiable with the issuing bank. If it is under $100,000 USD, it is known as a 「small CD」, while deposits over that amount are called 「jumbo CD」. A jumbo CD is somewhat more risky, because the FDIC cannot insure it, but is still a sound investment when made with a reputable bank. After the amount of deposit is decided, the term of the certificate of deposit is determined: this can range from six months to 20 years, and it is very important to understand the length of the term before signing paperwork, because you will pay a penalty for withdrawing funds early. Finally, an interest rate can be locked in. Depending on the market, it may be possible to secure a very favorable interest rate, although if the market improves, the interest rate will remain the same, unless a variable interest rate has been agreed upon. Generally, the longer the term, the better the interest rate.

There are a few things to be cautious of when one sets up a certificate of deposit. The first is whether the certificate of deposit is 「callable」 or not. If the certificate of deposit is callable, it means that the bank can terminate it, forcing the client to establish a new certificate of deposit, whether at that bank or another. Unfortunately, a certificate of deposit is usually called when interest rates drop, meaning that the client loses the high rate of interest that he or she has negotiated. Clients, of course, cannot call their certificates of deposit, which are locked in at the agreed upon rate and terms until the deposit matures. It is also important to understand how the interest rate works, including when it is applied and whether the interest is fixed or variable.

Finally it is important to make sure that you get a certificate of deposit from a reputation and FDIC or Federal Reserve insured source. If you are using a broker, check to make certain that you know which bank is issuing the certificate of deposit, and that the bank is insured. You should also check out the broker with the chamber of commerce, to make sure that he or she has not been involved in fraudulent activity. You can also check with the securities regulator for the state in which the broker works. When you do it safely and with care, a certificate of deposit is a sound long-term investment with a predictable yield.

New Words and Expressions

paperwork	*n.*	文件
principal	*n.*	本金
payroll	*n.*	發薪
deductible	*adj.*	可扣除的
reconcile	*v.*	調和
adhere	*v.*	堅持
vendor	*n.*	供應商
reimburse	*v.*	償還
Federal Reserve	*n.*	聯邦儲備委員會
withdraw	*v.*	提款
bankruptcy	*n.*	破產
endorse	*v.*	背書，簽署
jumbo	*adj.*	巨大的
reputation	*n.*	名聲，聲望

Notes

1. A checking account: it is a service provided by financial institutions which allows individuals and businesses to deposit money and withdraw fund from a federally-protected account.

2. A savings account: it typically refers to an account in which one places money to earn a small amount of interest.

3. A certificate of deposit: it is called a CD, which is a type of savings certificate.

4. Bank draft: it is a check drawn by a bank against funds deposited into its account at another bank, authorizing the second bank to make payment to the individual named in the draft.

Exercises

I. Choose the best answer to the following questions.

1. By using the checking account, which method can be used to check the balance of the account?

  A. Printed monthly statements of debits and credits.

  B. Use the ATM machines to check the current balance.

  C. Use online banking.

  D. All methods above.

2. Comparing the interest checking account and the savings account, which one of the following statements is correct?

  A. Interest checking accounts pay less interest.

  B. Savings accounts require higher minimum balance, about $1,000.

  C. Savings accounts charge high bank fees for using the accounts.

  D. Interest checking accounts charge $500 bank fees for using the accounts.

II. Translate the following sentences into Chinese.

1. Several types of deposit accounts are available. Checking accounts pay no interest and can be withdrawn upon demand.

2. A certificate of deposit can take a wide variety of forms which are negotiable with the issuing bank.

III. Read the text and answer the following questions.

1. Why is a jumbo CD more risky?

2. What is a checking account?

Types of Loans Granted by Commercial Banks

  Commercial banks are banking institutions that are geared more toward the lending of money to customers, rather than focusing on generating or raising money. A commercial bank accepts deposits to personal and corporate accounts, and then uses the combined strength of the deposits to finance loans for individuals and businesses. This is in contrast to an investment bank, which focuses on generated revenue through investments.

  The commercial bank will extend a number of different types of loans to customers. For individuals, a commercial bank may loan funds for the purchase of personal property, such as vehicles or homes. A commercial bank may also extend a personal loan to an individual for home improvements or consolidate a number of personal debt instruments. Loans of this type are usually extended with interest included, allowing the bank to cover the costs associated with extending the loan.

Business clients may also obtain loans from a commercial bank. The type of business loans that would be offered by a commercial institution would include funds to finance a payroll or to purchase operating supplies. However, if the funds were needed to effect a corporate realignment or restructuring, investment banks would more likely finance that type of business loan.

A commercial bank will also offer a wide range of savings programs for customers. Along with standard savings accounts, the commercial bank may also offer interest bearing checking accounts, certificates of deposit, and other savings strategies that are considered to provide a small but consistent return in exchange for doing business with the bank. The distinction between the functions of a commercial bank and those of an investment bank are not always clear. While the banking industry within the United States tends to operate with a clear division between the two types of banks, this is not always the case across the globe. Often, large international banking institutions will provide both commercial and investment banking services to their clients.

The name bank derives from the Italian word 「banco」(desk/bench), used during the Renaissance by Florentine bankers, who used to make their transactions above a desk covered by a green tablecloth. However, there are traces of banking activity even in ancient times. In fact, the word traces its origins back to the Ancient Roman Empire, where money lenders would set up their stalls in the middle of enclosed courtyards called macella on a long bench called a banco, from which the words banco and bank are derived. As a moneychanger, the merchant at the banco did not so much invest money as merely convert the foreign currency into the only legal tender in Rome—that of the Imperial Mint.

Commercial banks can provide types of loans to the customers:

Secured Loan

A secured loan is a loan in which the borrower pledges some asset as collateral.

Mortgage Loan

A mortgage loan is a very common type of debt instrument, used to purchase real estate under this arrangement; the money is used to purchase property. Commercial banks, however, are given security – a lien on the title to the house – until the mortgage is paid off in full. If the borrower defaults on the loan, the bank would have the legal right to repossess the house and sell it, to recover sums owing to it.

In the past, commercial banks have not been greatly interested in real estate loans and have placed only a relatively small percentage of assets in mortgages. As their name implies, such financial institutions secured their earning primarily from commercial and consumer loans and left the major task of home financing to others. However, due to changes in the banking laws and policies, commercial banks are increasingly active in home financing.

Changes in banking laws now allow commercial banks to make home mortgage loans on a more liberal basis than ever before. In acquiring mortgages on real estate, these institutions follow two main practices. First, some of the banks maintain active and well-organized departments whose primary function is to compete actively for real estate loans. In areas lacking specialized real estate financial institutions, these banks become the source for residential and farm mortgage loans. Second, the banks acquire mortgages by simply purchasing them from mortgage bankers or dealers.

In addition, dealer service companies, which were originally used to obtain car loans for permanent lenders such as commercial banks, wanted to broaden their activity beyond their local area. In recent years, however, such companies have concentrated on acquiring mobile home loans in volume for both commercial banks and savings and loan associations. Service companies obtain these loans from retail dealers, usually on a nonrecourse basis. Almost all bank/service company agreements contain a credit insurance policy that protects the lender if the consumer defaults.

The commercial bank offers a variety of mortgage programs with competitive rates and terms. The mortgage programs offered at the commercial bank are:

- fixed rate mortgage
- short-term balloon mortgage
- adjustable rate mortgage
- second mortgage

1. Fixed Rate Mortgage

A fixed rate mortgage is a mortgage in which the interest rate does not change during the entire term of the loan. The terms for fixed rate mortgages are usually 15 to 30 years. Other terms are available. The advantage of a fixed rate mortgage is that the interest rate will not increase. The disadvantage of a fixed rate mortgage occurs when interest rates drop substantially lower than your existing rate.

2. Short-term Balloon Mortgage

A short-term balloon mortgage, which involves small payments for a certain period of time and one large payment for the remaining amount of the principal at a time specified in the contract. The advantage of this type of loan is that the initial rate is usually lower than a normal fixed rate loan. The disadvantage of a balloon mortgage is that you may have to refinance or payoff the loan when the note matures. The interest rates at that time may be substantially higher.

3. Adjustable Rate Mortgage

An adjustable rate mortgage usually has a term of 30 years and interest rate that changes based on a standard rate index. Most adjustable rate mortgages have caps on how much the interest may increase or decrease. The initial rate is fixed for a specified period and thereafter has an adjustment interval of one year. The advantage of an adjustable rate mortgage is that the initial rate is usually lower than a traditional fixed rate mortgage. Also, the interest rate changes up or down depending on the financial conditions of the economy. This can be an advantage if interest rates remain the same or if there is a decline in the interest rates. The disadvantage of this type of loan is that the interest rate may increase.

4. Second Mortgage

A second mortgage is a second loan on the same property and home that is secured by a first mortgage loan. The interest you pay on a second mortgage may be tax deductible. (Consult your tax advisor to find out if you qualify for this deductible.)

5. Construction Loans

Build the home of your dreams with a construction loan from the commercial bank. The process is simple and easy; once the home is near completion the commercial bank will help you roll the loan over into permanent financing. All loans are subject to credit approval, acceptable collateral and available equity.

6. Unsecured Loan

Unsecured loans are monetary loans that are not secured by the borrower assets (i.e. no collateral is involved). These may be available from financial institutions under many different guises or marketing packages:

- credit card debt;
- personal loans;
- bank overdrafts;
- credit facilities or lines of credit;
- corporate bonds.

New Words and Expressions

revenue	n.	收入
personal property	n.	私有財產
division	n.	部門
savings	n.	儲蓄
courtyards	n.	庭院
merchant	n.	商人
pledge	n.	保證
real estate	n.	房地產，房產
mortgage	n.	抵押，抵押貸款
adjustable	a.	可調節的
construction	n.	建造物，構築（物）
overdraft	n.	透支

Notes

1. Secured loan: the borrower pledges some asset as collateral for the loan

2. Mortgage loan: the loan is used to purchase real estate. Under this arrangement, the money is used to purchase property.

3. Fixed rate mortgage: it is a mortgage in which the interest rate does not change during the entire term of the loan.

4. Short-term balloon mortgage: it involves small payments for a certain period of time and one large payment for the remaining amount of the principal at a time specified

in the contract.

5. Adjustable rate mortgage: it usually has a term of 30 years and interest rate that changes based on a standard rate index.

Exercises

I. Choose the best answer to the following questions.

1. Which of the following is the definition of the commercial bank?
    A. Banking institutions focus on lending of money to customers.
    B. Banking institutions focus on generating money from customers.
    C. Banking institutions provide consulting services to customers.
    D. Banking institutions help the customers to manage financial risks.
2. Which word does the name 「bank」 derive from?
    A. Bench
    B. Benson
    C. Banco
    D. Bancu
3. The credit card debt is a type of _____ loan.
    A. secured
    B. unsecured
    C. short-term balloon
    D. adjustable rate

II. Translate the following sentences into Chinese.

1. For individuals, a commercial bank may loan funds for the purchase of personal property, such as vehicles or homes. A commercial bank may also extend a personal loan to an individual for home improvements or consolidate a number of personal debt instruments.

2. In acquiring mortgages on real estate, these institutions follow two main practices. First, some of the banks maintain active and well-organized departments whose primary function is to compete actively for real estate loans. In areas lacking specialized real estate financial institutions, these banks become the source for residential and farm mortgage loans. Second, the banks acquire mortgage by simply purchasing them from mortgage bankers or dealers.

III. Read the text and answer the following questions.

1. What types of loan will commercial banks provide?
2. What are the advantages of the adjustable rate mortgage?

Part Three Regulation and Monetary Policies

Reading Comprehension

Monetary Policy

Monetary policy is the process by which the monetary authority of a country controls the supply of money, often targeting a rate of interest for the purpose of promoting economic growth and stability. The official goals usually include relatively stable prices and low unemployment. Monetary theory provides insight into how to craft optimal monetary policy. It is referred to as either being expansionary or contractionary, where an expansionary policy increases the total supply of money in the economy more rapidly than usual, and contractionary policy expands the money supply more slowly than usual or even shrinks it. Expansionary policy is traditionally used to try to combat unemployment in a recession by lowering interest rates in the hope that easy credit will entice businesses into expanding. Contractionary policy is intended to slow inflation in order to avoid the resulting distortions and deterioration of asset values.

Monetary policy is the process by which the government, central bank, or monetary authority of a country controls (i) the supply of money, (ii) availability of money, and (iii) cost of money or rate of interest to attain a set of objectives oriented towards the growth and stability of the economy.

Monetary policy rests on the relationship between the rate of interest in an economy, which is the price at which money can be borrowed, and the total supply of money. Monetary policy uses a variety of tools to control one or both of these, to influence outcomes like economic growth, inflation, exchange rates with other currencies and unemployment. Where currency is under a monopoly of issuance, or where there is a regulated system of issuing currency through banks which are tied to a central bank, the monetary authority has the ability to alter the money supply and thus influence the interest rate (to achieve policy goals).

It is important for policymakers to make credible announcements. If private agents (consumers and firms) believe that policymakers are committed to lowering inflation, they will anticipate future prices to be lower than otherwise (how those expectations are formed is an entirely different matter; compare for instance rational expectations with adaptive expectations). If an employee expects prices to be high in the future, he or she will draw up a wage contract with a high wage to match these prices. Hence, the expectation of lower wages is reflected in wage-setting behavior between employees and employers (lower wages since prices are expected to be lower) and since wages are in fact lower there is no demand pull inflation because employees are receiving a smaller wage and there is no cost push inflation because employers are paying out less in wages.

To achieve this low level of inflation, policymakers must have credible announcements; that is, private agents must believe that these announcements will reflect actual future policy. If an announcement about low-level inflation targets is made but not believed by private agents, wage-setting will anticipate high-level inflation and so wages will be higher and inflation will rise. A high wage will increase a consumer's demand (demand pull inflation) and a firm's costs (cost push inflation), so inflation rises. Hence, if a policymaker's announcements regarding monetary policy are not credible, policy will not have the desired effect.

If policymakers believe that private agents anticipate low inflation, they have an incentive to adopt an expansionist monetary policy (where the marginal benefit of increasing economic output outweighs the marginal cost of inflation); however, assuming private agents have rational expectations, they know that policymakers have this incentive. Hence, private agents know that if they anticipate low inflation, an expansionist policy will be adopted that causes a rise in inflation. Consequently, (unless policymakers can make their announcement of low inflation credible,) private agents expect high inflation. This anticipation is fulfilled through adaptive expectation (wage-setting behavior); so, there is higher inflation (without the benefit of increased output). Hence, unless credible announcements can be made, expansionary monetary policy will fail.

Announcements can be made credible in various ways. One is to establish an independent central bank with low inflation targets (but no output targets). Hence, private agents know that inflation will be low because it is set by an independent body.

Central banks can be given incentives to meet targets (for example, larger budgets, a wage bonus for the head of the bank) to increase their reputation and signal a strong commitment to a policy goal. Reputation is an important element in monetary policy implementation. But the idea of reputation should not be confused with commitment.

While a central bank might have a favorable reputation due to good performance in conducting monetary policy, the same central bank might not have chosen any particular form of commitment (such as targeting a certain range for inflation). Reputation plays a crucial role in determining how much markets would believe the announcement of a particular commitment to a policy goal but both concepts should not be assimilated. Also, note that under rational expectations, it is not necessary for the policymaker to have established its reputation through past policy actions; as an example, the reputation of the head of the central bank might be derived entirely from his or her ideology, professional background, public statements, etc.

In fact it has been argued that to prevent some pathologies related to the time inconsistency of monetary policy implementation (in particular excessive inflation), the head of a central bank should have a larger distaste for inflation than the rest of the economy on average. Hence the reputation of a particular central bank is not necessarily tied to past performance, but rather to particular institutional arrangements that the markets can use to form inflation expectations.

Despite the frequent discussion of credibility as it relates to monetary policy, the exact meaning of credibility is rarely defined. Such lack of clarity can serve to lead policy away from what is believed to be the most beneficial. For example, capability to serve the public interest is one definition of credibility often associated with central banks. The reliability with which a central bank keeps its promises is also a common definition. While everyone most likely agrees a central bank should not lie to the public, wide disagreement exists on how a central bank can best serve the public interest. Therefore, lack of definition can lead people to believe they are supporting one particular policy of credibility when they are really supporting another.

New Words and Expressions

authority	*n.* 權利，當局
announcement	*n.* 宣布

adaptive	*adj.* 能適應的，適合的
inflation	*n.* 通貨膨脹
marginal cost	*n.* 邊際成本
rational	*adj.* 理智的，合理的
benefit	*n.* 利益，好處
credible	*adj.* 可信的，可靠的
implementation	*n.* 實施，貫徹
confuse	*v.* 使……糊涂
associate	*v.* 聯繫，聯想
inconsistency	*n.* 不一致，前後矛盾
definition	*n.* 定義
distaste	*n.* 不喜歡，厭惡

Notes

1. Monetary policy is the process by which the monetary authority of a country controls the supply of money, often targeting a rate of interest for the purpose of promoting economic growth and stability.

2. Inflation: In economics, inflation is a rise in the general level of prices of goods and services in an economy over a period of time.

3. Marginal cost: In economics and finance, marginal cost is the change in the total cost that arises when the quantity produced changes by one unit. That is, it is the cost of producing one more unit of goods.

4. The exchange rate (also known as a foreign-exchange rate, forex rate, FX rate) between two currencies is the rate at which one currency will be exchanged for another. It is also regarded as the value of one country's currency in terms of another currency.

Exercises

I. Choose the best answer to the following question.

Monetary policy includes the process to control _____.

    A. the supply of money

    B. availability of money

C. rate of interest
D. all of the above

II. Translate the following sentences into Chinese.

1. Monetary policy is the process by which the government, central bank, or monetary authority of a country controls (ⅰ) the supply of money, (ⅱ) availability of money, and (ⅲ) cost of money or rate of interest to attain a set of objectives oriented towards the growth and stability of the economy.

2. If policymakers believe that private agents anticipate low inflation, they have an incentive to adopt an expansionist monetary policy (where the marginal benefit of increasing economic output outweighs the marginal cost of inflation); however, assuming private agents have rational expectations, they know that policymakers have this incentive.

III. Read the text and answer the following questions.

1. In what ways can announcements be made credible?
2. Discuss the functions of monetary policy.

Chinese Policy Makers will Boost Domestic Demand and Fight Inflation

Chinese leaders are pledging to seek stable and more balanced growth while fighting inflation, ending a top - level economic planning session without major shifts in policy. Above, a vegetable vender arranges her merchandise at a street stall in Shanghai Wednesday. The statement on Wednesday comes as Chinese authorities have shifted their focus away from controlling inflation—their top priority over the past year—and toward insulating China from Europe's economic troubles, which have already hurt Chinese export growth.

China will focus on expanding domestic demand to counter a slowing global economy, the government said in a statement released after a meeting of the central economic work conference, an annual gathering of top policy makers and political leaders during which economic policy is planned for the coming year. 「This memo is definitely more pro - growth than the one issued a year ago,」 Bank of America Merrill Lynch economist Lu Ting said in a note to clients.

「We believe that compared with this year, fiscal policy in next year will be more proactive and monetary policy will be eased on the margin,」 he wrote. China's leaders said in the statement that global economic risks「have clearly risen.」「Over the past year, world economic growth has slowed, growth of international trade has moderated, there has been severe international financial volatility,」the statement said.

The global economic environment will remain「extremely severe and complicated」next year, and in response, Chinese policy makers will boost domestic demand and social spending that will increase the「inclusiveness」of economic development, the statement said.「The focus on expanding domestic demand should be more on protecting and improving people's livelihoods,」it said.

Financial adviser Yin Long says her Chinese heritage has helped grow her business and tap into a profitable market. She gives tips to advisers looking to reach Chinese-Americans. China will keep credit growth at reasonable levels and ensure sufficient funding for railway development, it said. China's railway build out has been tripped up by a deadly high-speed train accident in July and allegations of corruption within the Railway Ministry, drying up funding for some projects.

Also Wednesday, the People's Bank of China released data showing that lending fell slightly in November compared with October but remained elevated. Chinese financial institutions issued 562. 2 billion yuan ($88. 24 billion) of new yuan loans in November, the central bank said, down from 586. 8 billion yuan in October but above economists' median forecast of 555 billion yuan. Lending in both October and November was higher than the monthly average in the third quarter, which saw new yuan loans average around 500 billion yuan a month. This shows authorities have been encouraging lending as credit growth typically falls toward the end of the year, analysts said.

UBS economist Wang Tao said she expects full-year bank lending to be around 7. 4 trillion yuan, in line with a 7 trillion yuan to 7. 5 trillion yuan unofficial target that analysts believe the central bank has set. For next year, the new yuan loans will be around 8 trillion yuan, Ms. Wang added. China next year will also push forward with structural tax cuts, reform of business-income taxes and value-added taxes, and experimental property-tax reforms, the statement from Chinese leaders said, without elaborating. The statement repeated language on the yuan that has been used for years, saying it will keep the exchange rate basically stable while continuing exchange-rate reform. The country will also deepen market-oriented interest-rate reform, it said, without giving a specific time line for the long-awaited liberalization of interest rates.

New Words and Expressions

merchandise	n. 商品，貨物
insulate	vt. 使隔離，使孤立；使絕緣，使隔熱
proactive	adj. 積極主動的；前攝的；主動出擊的；先發制人的
moderate	vt. 使和緩；主持；節制
inclusiveness	n. 包容性
allegation	n. 指控；陳述，主張；宣稱
corruption	n. 腐敗；貪污；賄賂
elaborate	vi. 詳盡說明，變得複雜
oriented	adj. 導向的，定向的
liberalization	n. 自由化

Notes

1. Fiscal policy: It is the use of government revenue collection (mainly taxes) and expenditure (spending) to influence the economy. The two main instruments of fiscal policy are changes in the level, composition of taxation, and government spending in various sectors.

2. Corruption: It is a form of dishonest or unethical conduct by a person entrusted with a position of authority, often to acquire personal benefit. Corruption may include many activities including bribery and embezzlement, though it may also involve practices that are legal in many countries.

3. income tax: It is a government levy (tax) imposed on individuals or entities (taxpayers) that varies with the income or profits (taxable income) of the taxpayer. Details vary widely by jurisdiction. Many jurisdictions refer to income tax on business entities as companies tax or corporate tax.

4. value-added tax: It also called goods and services tax (GST) is a popular way of implementing a consumption tax in Europe, Japan, and many other countries. It differs from the sales tax in that taxes are applied to the difference between the seller-purchased price and the resale price. This is accomplished by taking full tax on all sales, but refunding the tax difference to the sellers.

5. market-oriented: It is a term that refers to the character of business manage-

ment and operations that are geared to satisfying demands of the consumer marketplace in terms of product, price and distribution. It is also a term used in economics to describe economic policies that favor business and its activities, promoting ever increasing sales to consumers.

Exercises

I. Choose the best answer to the following questions.

1. According to the author, what is major economic planning in China over the past years?

   A. liberalization of interest rates
   B. tax cuts
   C. reducing inflation
   D. expanding domestic demand

2. Why China plans to focus on expanding domestic demand?

   A. rising inflation rate
   B. global economic risks
   C. Fall of lending
   D. Fall of Chinese export growth

3. China will issue the _____ fiscal policies and _____ monetary policies to boost social spending.

   A. tighter, looser
   B. looser, looser
   C. tighter, tighter
   D. Looser, tighter

4. According to the article, amount of the monthly average in the third quarter is about _____.

   A. less than 586.8 billion yuan
   B. less than 562.2 billion yuan
   C. less than 555 billion yuan
   D. less than 500 billion yuan

5. Chinese authorities will enhance reform with the following EXCEPT _____.

   A. rise the business – income taxes

B. deepen market – oriented interest – rate reform
C. keep the exchange rate basically stable
D. rise the bank lending

Chapter Three: Investment System

Part One Investment Bank

Reading Comprehension

Investment Banks and Investment Bankers

By Bolun Miao

In 2008, the biggest financial crisis after the Great Depression broke out and the world economy has struggled until now. Once again, many investment banks in the Wall Street stand in the centre of the storm. Thus, investment banks and investment bankers' sky-high salaries tend to be a very debatable topic recently.

An investment bank is a financial institution doing underwriting of securities, issuance securities and shares, helping companies involved in mergers and acquisitions and providing ancillary services such as market making, trading of derivatives, trading in the secondary market and the future market, etc. Investment banking is sometimes misunderstood because we often use 「bank」 as a depository institution, known as savings bank or commercial bank, which accepts deposits and makes loans or invests money from the deposits. Investment banks in US are different from depository institutions, especially after the *Glass-Steagall Act* was established in 1933 (until 1999). While in Europe, most banks such as Deutsche Bank and Credit Suisse are doing mixed banking activities, both investment banking and depository activity.

From beginning, the Italian business men invented the Bank's Acceptance Bill. Then, as the industrial economy grew sharply in 18th century, many merchant banks appeared in Europe and pushed the whole Europe to step forward. During the American Civil War, the trading in government bonds and railway bonds tended to be the origin of investment banking in the US. After the World War II, investment banks were no longer doing the pure investment banking; they paid more attention on enterprises investment and fund raising. Nowadays, before 2008, the derivatives were extremely popular in investment banking. However, as the derivatives trading is in margin system, it has a high leverage ratio; it has high payoffs with high risk.

In 17th, Sep. 2011, a protest movement broke out called Occupy Wall Street. One reason the protesters held is that investment bankers get too high salaries and too many bonuses. Going into 2011, starting salaries for investment banking positions with a bachelor's degree should range from £ 63,000 to £ 82,000 after bonus. Starting salaries with an MBA degree range after bonus from £ 57,000 to £ 114,000. These salaries vary with firms and with the region of the country bankers are in. Bonuses typically would be 10% ~ 50% of salary to start and can move to one to three times salary later. Lately, salaries have increasingly included an equity component which may not be liquid for up to three years, although as an analyst people would typically be sheltered from this. This is good for the banks because it makes it much harder for people to move around. Most individuals complain that bankers get too many notes.

It is not fair to bankers. To begin with, as a banker, the average time on working is approximately 100 hours per week. Bankers, indeed, earn almost the highest salary around the world, but they also have nearly the biggest working pressure and longest working hours. If a young banker with bachelor degree earns £ 70,000 after bonus, which is higher than average, in the first year, and assume that he has no vacation and works 100 hours per week, nearly 14 hours per day, then he works 5,110 hours per year, and earns £ 13.69 per hour. Secondly, considering the investment bank as a firm, employees hire employers, paying them by profits they make. It is fair and incentive to all employers. In an investment bank, if a banker brings £ 1,000,000 profit to the company, undoubtedly, employers should give a large amount of money in order to at least show respect to the banker and give him an incentive to stay in the company. Unquestionably, investment banking is a field where people can normally make that big amount of profit for the company. Thirdly, because of the growth in economy, more and more companies want to be listed in order to expand the size. Anyway, companies need the professional help and advice from investment banks; and bankers will earn a large amount of commission. Except stocks, futures and foreign exchange derivatives, many new and complex derivatives are invented by investment banks, few to individuals but more to corporations and countries. For example, in 1994-1995, Morgan Stanley invented two different derivatives about exchange rate and sold them to Mexico and India. Investment banks focus on big corporations and even countries; undoubtedly, their payoffs cannot be tiny, as well as their employers. Not only Morgan Stanley got payoff in trading with nations. Goldman helped Greece to cover 1 billion Euros liabilities by a way called 「financial innovation」; Greece finally became a member of European Union. According to news, Goldman got 300 million dollars from his help in 2001. It is acceptable that bankers earn more notes.

As more and more countries open their financial markets, it will become a global financial battlefield. Only the strong can survive. While American bankers never stop harassing the Yens, Euros, British Pounds and Chinese Yuan, who can finally survive?

New Words and Expressions

Great Depression	大蕭條
struggle	*v.* 搏鬥；奮鬥；努力
debatable	*adj.* 可爭辯的；成問題的；未定的
mergers	*n.* （公司、組織等的）合併，歸並
acquisition	*n.* （對公司的）收購，併購
merchant	*adj.* 商人的；商業的
Occupy Wall Street	「佔領華爾街」
derivatives	*n.* 衍生性金融商品；派生物，引出物
exchange rate	匯率
note	*n.* 紙幣，鈔票
payoff	*n.* 報酬；結清，算清

Notes

1. Investment bank: is a financial institution that assists individuals, corporations, and governments in raising capital by underwriting and/or acting as the client's agent in the issuance of securities. An investment bank may also assist companies involved in mergers and acquisitions and provide ancillary services such as market making, trading of derivatives and equity securities, and FICC services (fixed income instruments, currencies, and commodities).

2. Great Depression: a severe worldwide economic depression in the decade preceding World War II. The timing of the Great Depression varied across nations, but in most countries it started in 1930 and lasted until the late 1930s or middle 1940s. It was the longest, most widespread, and deepest depression of the 20th century.

3. Underwriting: carrying out a detailed investigation of the risk involved in making a loan to a particular borrower, especially by a bank.

4. Acceptance Bill: or BA, is a promised future payment, or time draft, which is accepted and guaranteed by a bank and drawn on a deposit at the bank. The banker's acceptance specifies the amount of money, the date, and the person to which the payment is due. After acceptance, the draft becomes an unconditional liability of the bank. But the holder of the draft can sell (exchange) it for cash at a discount to a buyer who is willing to wait until the maturity date for the funds in the deposit.

5. Foreign exchange: instruments used for international payments, i. e., currency, checks, drafts, and bills of exchange.

6. Occupy Wall Street: (OWS) was the name given to a protest movement that began on September 17, 2011, in Zuccotti Park, located in New York City's Wall Street financial district.

7. Morgan Stanley: (NYSE: MS) is an American multinational financial services corporation headquartered in the Morgan Stanley Building, Midtown Manhattan, New York City. Morgan Stanley operates in 42 countries, and has more than 1,300 offices and 60,000 employees. The company reports US $ 304 billion in assets under management or supervision.

Exercises

I. Choose the best answer to the following questions.

1. Which of the following is not the function of the investment bank?

    A. Trading of derivatives.   B. Market making.

    C. Issue currency.   D. Underwriting of securities.

2. Which of the following statements is not true?

    A. Usually, investment banks provide services and trade in the secondary market and the future market.

    B. People usually use the investment bank as a depository institution.

C. However, derivatives trading has a high leverage ratio and high payoffs with high risk.

D. More and more companies want to be listed because of the desire for scale-up.

II. Translate the following sentences into Chinese.

1. An investment bank is a financial institution doing underwriting of securities, issuance securities and shares, helping companies involved in mergers and acquisitions and providing ancillary services such as market making, trading of derivatives, trading in the secondary market and the future market.

2. After the World War II, investment banks were no longer doing the pure investment banking; they paid more attention on enterprises investment and fund raising. Nowadays, before 2008, the derivatives were extremely popular in investment banking.

3. Not only Morgan Stanley got payoff in trading with nations. Goldman helped Greece to cover 1 billion Euros liabilities by a way called 「financial innovation」; Greece finally became a member of European Union. According to news, Goldman got 300 million dollars from his help in 2001. It is acceptable that bankers earn more notes.

III. Read the text and answer the following questions.

1. What is the investment bank?
2. What are the main tasks of an investment bank?
3. During the American Civil War, what were the investment banks doing?
4. Why is it not fair that most individuals complain that bankers get too many notes?

Global Investment Banks Try China – Again

By Wu Ying, Caixin Online

BEIJING – Shaking off the sort of jitters teenagers feel on a first date, global investment banks are getting bolder about business opportunities in the Chinese financial services sector.

J. P. Morgan (NYSE: JPM) China Chief Executive officer Fang Fang told reporters March 9 that the U. S. -based bank hoped to establish a securities joint venture in China as soon as possible and 「serve domestic investors and issuers, helping them enter China's capital market」.

A day earlier, Royal Bank of Scotland said it would apply for a joint venture securities license in China, adding that it had settled on a partner.

Several other foreign investors similarly announced partners for hoped-for joint venture licenses in recent months, including Australia's largest investment bank Macquarie Group Ltd., which signed a memorandum of understanding with China's Hengtai Securities Co. Ltd.

In another pending deal, Citigroup and Central China Securities recently signed a letter of intent for a joint venture that's now seeking regulatory approval. And Morgan Stanley is about to conclude a deal to sell its stake in China International Capital Corp. Ltd. (CICC), which is expected to leave the U.S. company free to launch a new joint venture with China Fortune Securities Ltd.

An exception to the flurry of foreign ambition is U.S.-based Goldman Sachs, which insists on using the same compliance requirements in China that it uses in other countries, such as wealth disclosure. Because it won't relax standards, the firm has lost a number of potential clients that refused to open their books.

International investment banks that don't mind following China's procedures, though, lean toward modest domestic partners. They also have to contend with a regulatory environment that's slowed foreign interests in the past.

「From a strategic standpoint, global investment banks are not satisfied with acting as financial investors and having no substantial controlling position,」said an industry analyst. 「Seeking out a relatively weak partner is perhaps their best choice.」

Money Makers

Brokerages serving China's A-share market are considered 「easy」 money makers because they require little expertise but yield high returns.

Global investment banks, however, usually focus on mature markets and give priority to institutional investors, giving little thought to retail markets and individual investors. CICC, for example, has since its start in 1995, focused primarily on investment banking without venturing far into brokerage services.

「Over 80% of the U.S. market for brokerage services is from institutional investors,」explained Gao Hua Securities chief executive officer Zhang Xing. 「There is no need for networks or commission wars.」

「On the contrary, 80% of China's market comes from retail investors,」he said.

「Competitors offer discount commissions. Thus, average profits in the industry are quite low.」

And the strong performance of China's stock market in recent years has improved brokerage revenues, so that today they are a powerful source of financial-sector profit.

「People are gradually realizing that the retail market can still be highly profitable in China,」said Qi Li, chief strategist at Zhongde Securities.

「We need to take another look at the status of retail brokerage services,」Qi said.「Even though there will inevitably be intense competition in this sector with local securities traders, the industry is immense, and in the end there is still great profit potential.」

「The market in China is different, so the strategic focus should be different as well.」

Regulatory Caution

At the same time, securities regulators have been cautious about opening up China's financial services market to foreign capital.

Chinese firms tied to joint ventures have complained about foreign partners holding dominant positions. Against this backdrop, global banks have been repeatedly held back by Chinese rules and regulators.

Regulators in recent years have focused on opening up investment banking options while restricting brokerage businesses.

In late 2007, regulations for securities trading were loosened so that foreign investors could buy shares in listed domestic securities firms on the secondary market. The rules said a single foreign investor could not own more than 20% of a Chinese company, and total shares owned by all of a company's foreign investors could not exceed 25%. This paved the way for foreign investors to become shareholders of full-service, fully licensed securities firms.

However, due to relatively high prices for listed securities companies – and because foreign investors would not likely get management rights – no deals have been made since the policy was announced three years ago. And the profit models of existing securities joint ventures are still centered on investment banking.

Securities joint ventures on the A-share market are subject to relatively stringent net capital requirements. In addition, Zhang said,「compliance requirements from within the company can also greatly impede business development.」

Chinese securities companies have access to ample cash and net capital from the market. Raising money by issuing shares is fairly easy.

One of the largest Chinese securities firm, CITIC Securities Co. Ltd. , reported about 35 billion yuan ($5.1 billion) in net capital last June, while CICC reported end-2009 net capital of 4.4 billion yuan.

But fund-raising is more difficult for joint ventures because it requires coordination by Chinese and foreign shareholders, limiting their options.

New Words and Expressions

joint venture	合資企業
issuer	n. 發行商
memorandum	n. 備忘錄，便箋，函
pending	adj. 未決的，未定的，待定的
disclosure	n. 公開；洩露，揭露
brokerage	n. 經紀業；佣金，手續費，經紀費
A-share market	A 股市場
yield	n. 產量，產額；投資的收益
commission	n. 佣金，手續費
retail	adj. 零售的
revenue	n. 稅收，收入，收益
discount	v. 折扣，貼現率，貼現
potential	adj. 潛在的，有可能的
strategic	adj. 戰略性的，有戰略意義的；至關重要的
dominant	adj. 占優勢的，統治的，支配的
share	n. 股票
list	v. 上市
ample cash	充足的現金
net capital	資本淨值

Notes

1. Capital market: financial markets for the buying and selling of long-term debt-

or equity-backed securities. These markets channel the wealth of savers to those who can put it to long-term productive use, such as companies or governments making long-term investments. Financial regulators, such as the UK's Bank of England (BOE) or the U.S. Securities and Exchange Commission (SEC), oversee the capital markets in their jurisdictions to protect investors against fraud, among other duties.

2. Goldman Sachs: is an American multinational investment banking firm that engages in global investment banking, securities, investment management, and other financial services primarily with institutional clients.

3. A-share: a designation for a 「class」 of common or preferred stock. A-shares of common or preferred stock typically have enhanced voting rights or other benefits compared to the other forms of shares that may have been created. The equity structure, or how many types of shares are offered, is determined by the corporate charter.

4. Secondary market: also called aftermarket, is the financial market in which previously issued financial instruments such as stock, bonds, options, and futures are bought and sold. Another frequent usage of 「secondary market」 is to refer to loans which are sold by a mortgage bank to investors such as Fannie Mae and Freddie Mac.

Exercises

I. Choose the best answer to the following questions.

1. Which statement is true?
    A. Global investment banks are eager to enter China for China is a mature market.
    B. Unlike business in other nations, retail markets are more important for the global investment banks in China.
    C. When the global investment banks get into China, they would provide services to institutional investors.
    D. Global investment banks care little about individual investors in China.

2. Most global investment banks would access to China by _____.
    A. finding an influential partner in China
    B. finding a relatively weaker partner in China
    C. approaching an authority
    D. establishing an office of their own

金融英語閱讀 Financial English Reading

II. Translate the following sentences into Chinese.

1. International investment banks that don't mind following China's procedures, though, lean toward modest domestic partners. They also have to contend with a regulatory environment that's slowed foreign interests in the past.

2. Global investment banks, however, usually focus on mature markets and give priority to institutional investors, giving little thought to retail markets and individual investors. CICC, for example, has since its start in 1995, focused primarily on investment banking without venturing far into brokerage services.

3. Chinese firms tied to joint ventures have complained about foreign partners holding dominant positions. Against this backdrop, global banks have been repeatedly held back by Chinese rules and regulators.

III. Read the text and answer the following questions.

1. What is Chinese securities regulators' attitude to global investment banks' getting into China?

2. What is the result of the regulations for securities trading loosened in late 2007?

3. Why do investment banks realize that the retail market can be highly profitable in China?

4. What is the meaning of the statement that Goldman Sachs has lost a number of potential clients that refused to open their books?

Part Two Investment Instruments

Reading Comprehension

China Sells More US T-Bonds

By Shangguan Zhoudong, China Daily

China sold more US treasury bonds in April than any time in at least seven years, a signal that the nation may be diversifying the world's largest foreign-exchange reserves, Shanghai Securities News reported today.

Statistics from the US Treasury Department show that China sold a net US $5.8

billion of T-bonds, the first drop in holdings since October 2005. Japan remains the largest holder of US T-bonds, with its holdings reaching US $614.8 billion in April, according to the statistics.

China remained the second-largest holder of US T-bonds, as its stake fell to US $414.0 billion in April from US $419.8 billion in March this year. The United States had US $4.4 trillion of tradable bonds in April.

As an effort to diversify its for-exchange investment channels, China also established a new specialized foreign exchange investment company named the State Investment Company to focus on investing in high-return bonds, stock markets, real estate and private equities. Analysts estimate the company may start with US $200 billion in capital.

「China's newly-added forex reserves through trade surplus are enough to make high-yield investments, and China may not and need not use the US $1.2 trillion forex reserves,」said Sun Mingchun, an economist with Lehman Brothers.「China won't sell a large amount of US T-bonds even if it wants to sell.」Marc Chandler, Chief Currency Strategist at Brown Brothers Harriman & Co, said that there's no clear sign Chinese investors are going to dump US T-bonds, noting that Chinese officials have said they have no intention of doing anything that would devalue their holdings.

Treasury Secretary Henry Paulson and Federal Reserve Chairman Ben S. Bernanke have repeatedly played down concern of a sell-off in T-bond holdings by foreign investors. Paulson noted again this week that China's holdings amount to about one day's worth of trading in the T-bond market.

Greg Anderson, director of currency strategy at ABN Amro Bank NV, said he was unconcerned about the decline in China's holdings of US T-bonds because the country is still buying US assets, providing support for the dollar. Statistics from the Treasury Department also show that global investors in April this year sold a net US $28.2 billion of bonds, with their holdings down to US $2.17 trillion from US $2.19 trillion at the end of March.

To attract more investments in US dollar assets, Treasury Deputy Secretary Robert Kimmitt plans to lobby China and Russia to keep investing in the US on his trips to Moscow and Beijing next week. He said he plans a similar message on upcoming visits to Japan, South Korea and the Middle East.

New Words and Expressions

foreign-exchange reserves	外匯儲備
T-bonds	債券
statistics	n. 統計，統計資料，統計數字
real estate	n. 不動產，土地；房地產
surplus	adj. 過剩的；多餘的
dump	v. 傾銷
devalue	v. 使（貨幣）貶值；降低（某事物）的價值
sell-off	n. 證券的跌價；廉價拋售；出清存貨
lobby	v. 對……進行遊說；陳情

Notes

1. Foreign-exchange reserves: also called forex reserves or FX reserves, are assets held by central banks and monetary authorities, usually in different reserve currencies, mostly the United States dollar, and to a lesser extent the euro, the United Kingdom pound sterling, and the Japanese yen, and used to back its liabilities, e.g., the local currency issued, and the various bank reserves deposited with the central bank, by the government or financial institutions.

2. Treasury bonds: also called T-bonds, or the long bond, have the longest maturity, from twenty years to thirty years. They have a coupon payment every six months like T-notes, and are commonly issued with maturity of thirty years. The secondary market is highly liquid, so the yield on the most recent T-bond offering was commonly used as a proxy for long-term interest rates in general.

3. Lehman Brothers: was a global financial services firm. Before declaring bankruptcy in 2008, Lehman was the fourth-largest investment bank in the US (behind Goldman Sachs, Morgan Stanley, and Merrill Lynch), doing business in investment banking, equity and fixed-income sales and trading (especially U.S. Treasury securities), research, investment management, private equity, and private banking.

Exercises

I. Choose the best answer to the following questions.

1. Which country is the largest holder of US T-bonds?

   A. China	B. UK

   C. Japan	D. Russia

2. To attract more investments in US dollar assets, which country does Robert Kimmitt plan to convince to invest?

   A. China	B. South Korea

   C. Japan	D. Singapore

II. Read the text and answer the following questions.

1. Why was Greg Anderson not concerned about the decline in China's holdings of US T-bonds?

2. What is the useful way for China to diversify its for-exchange investment channels?

3. Why won't China sell a large amount of US T-bonds even if it wants to do so?

III. Translate the article into Chinese.

How to Buy Bonds

Most bond transactions can be completed through a full service or discount brokerage. You can also open an account with a bond broker, but be warned that most bond brokers require a minimum initial deposit of $5,000. If you cannot afford this amount, we suggest looking at a mutual fund that specializes in bonds (a bond fund). Some financial institutions will provide their clients with the service of transacting government securities. However, if your bank doesn't provide this service and you do not have a brokerage account, you can purchase government bonds through a government agency (this is true in most countries). All transactions and interest payments are done electronically. If you do decide to purchase a bond through your broker, he or she may tell you that the trade is commission free. Don't be fooled. What typically happens is that the broker will mark up the price slightly; this markup is really the same as a commission. To make sure that you are not being taken advantage of, simply look up the latest quote for bond and determine whether the markup is acceptable.

Reading Comprehension

Stocks and Stock Exchanges

In business and finance, a share of stock means a share of ownership in a corporation. In the plural, stocks is often used as a synonym for shares especially in the United States, but it is less commonly used that way outside of North America.

A stock exchange is an organization that provides a marketplace for either physical or virtual trading shares where investors may buy and sell shares of a wide range of companies. Most stocks are traded on exchanges, which are places where buyers and sellers meet and decide on a price. Some exchanges are physical locations where transactions are carried out on a trading floor. You've probably seen pictures of a trading floor, in which traders are wildly throwing their arms up, waving yelling, and signaling to each other. The other type of exchange is virtual, composed of a network of computers where trades are made electronically.

The stock market is driven solely by supply and demand. The number of shares of stock available for sale dictates the supply and the number of shares that investors want to buy dictates the demand. It's important to understand that for every share that is purchased, there is someone on the other end selling that share (or vice versa). When people's views of the stock market or individual stocks change (which can be driven by economic fundamentals, consumer confidence, fear of terrorism, or company earnings), the demand for stock changes. This also causes the prices to change. For example, if people in general believe that the economy is growing, they become more optimistic and want to own more stock. This increases the demand for stock. At the same time, since people are selling less stock, it also decreases the supply of stock for sale. Both of these factors cause the average stock price to rise.

The purpose of a stock market is to facilitate the exchange of securities between buyers and sellers, reducing the risks of investing. Just imagine how difficult it would be to sell shares if you had to call around the neighborhood trying to find a buyer. Really, a stock market is nothing more than a super-sophisticated farmers' market linking buyers and sellers.

Before we go on, we should distinguish between the primary market and the secondary market. The primary market is where securities are created (by means of an

IPO) while, in the secondary market, investors trade previously-issued securities without the involvement of the issuing-companies. The secondary market is what people are referring to when they talk about the stock market. It is important to understand that the trading of a company's stock does not directly involve that company.

The New York Stock Exchange

The most prestigious exchange in the world is the New York Stock Exchange (NYSE). The 「Big Board」 was founded over 200 years ago in 1792 with the signing of the Buttonwood Agreement by 24 New York City stockbrokers and merchants. Currently the NYSE, with stocks like General Electric, McDonald's, Citigroup, Coca-Cola, Gillette and Walmart, is the market of choice for the largest companies in America.

The NYSE is the first type of exchange (as we referred to above), where much of the trading is done face-to-face on trading floor. This is also referred to as a listed exchange. Orders come in through brokerage firms that are members of the exchange and flow down to floor brokers who go to a specific spot on the floor where the stock trades. At this location, known as the trading post, there is a specific person known as the specialist whose job is to match buyers and sellers. Prices are determined using an auction method: the current price at which someone is willing to sell. Once a trade has been made, the details are sent back to the brokerage firm, who then notifies the investor who placed the order. Although there is human contact in this process, don't think that the NYSE is still in the Stone Age: computers play a huge role in the process.

The NASDAQ

The second type of exchange is the virtual sort called an over-the-counter (OTC) market, of which the NASDAQ is the most popular. These markets have no central location or floor brokers whatsoever. Trading is done through a computer and telecommunications network of dealers. It used to be that the largest companies were listed only on the NYSE while all other second tier stocks traded on the other exchanges. The tech boom of the late 1990s changed all this; now the NASDAQ is home to several big technology companies such as Microsoft, Cisco, Intel, Dell and Oracle. This has resulted in the NASDAQ becoming a serious competitor to the NYSE. On the NASDAQ brokerages act as market makers for various stocks. A market maker provides continuous bid and ask prices within a prescribed percentage spread for shares for which they are designated to make a market. They may match up buyers and sellers directly but usually they will maintain an inventory of shares to meet demands of investors.

Other Exchanges

The third largest exchange in the U.S. is the American Stock Exchange (AMEX). The AMEX used to be an alternative to the NYSE, but that role has since been filled by the NASDAQ. In fact, the National Association of Securities Dealers (NASD), which is the parent of NASDAQ, bought the AMEX in 1988. Almost all trading now on the AMEX is in small-cap stocks and derivatives.

There are many stock exchanges located in just about every country or district around the world. American markets are undoubtedly the largest, but they still represent only a fraction of total investment around the globe. The two other main financial hubs are London, home of the London Stock Exchange, and Hong Kong, home of the Hong Kong Stock Exchange. The last place worth mentioning is the over-the-counter bulletin board (OTCBB). The NASDAQ is an over-the-counter market, but the term commonly refers to small public companies that don't meet the listing requirements of any of the regulated markets, including the NASDAQ. The OTCBB is home to penny stocks because there is little to no regulation. This makes investing in an OTCBB stock very risky.

These stock exchanges provide facilities for the issue and redemption of securities as well as other financial instruments and capital events including the payment of income and dividends. The securities traded on a stock exchange include: shares issued by companies, unit trusts and other pooled investment products and bonds. A stock exchange is often the most important component of a stock market. Supply and demand in the stock market is driven by various factors which, as in all free markets, affect the price of stocks.

New Words and Expressions

exchange	*n.*	交換，交易；交易所
optimistic	*adj.*	樂觀的，樂觀主義的
primary market		一級市場
secondary market		二級市場
speculator	*n.*	投機商
broker	*n.*	經紀人

trading floor		交易場地
listed exchange		上市交易
over the counter		場外交易
inventory	n.	存貨總值
dividend	n.	紅利，股息，利息

Notes

1. Primary market: a market that issues new securities on an exchange. Companies, governments and other groups obtain financing through debt or equity based securities. Primary markets are facilitated by underwriting groups, which consist of investment banks that will set a beginning price range for a given security and then oversee its sale directly to investors.

2. Secondary market: a market where investors purchase securities or assets from other investors, rather than from issuing companies themselves. The national exchanges, such as the New York Stock Exchange and the NASDAQ are secondary markets.

3. Over-the-counter (OTC): a security traded in some context other than on a formal exchange such as the NYSE, TSX, AMEX, etc. The phrase「over-the-counter」can be used to refer to stocks that trade via a dealer network as opposed to on a centralized exchange. It also refers to debt securities and other financial instruments such as derivatives, which are traded through a dealer network.

4. Bulls: an investor who thinks the market, a specific security or an industry will rise.

5. Bears: an investor who believes that a particular security or market is headed downward. Bears attempt to profit from a decline in prices. Bears are generally pessimistic about the state of a given market.

6. Stockbroker: a regulated professional individual, usually associated with a brokerage firm or broker-dealer, who buys and sells shares and other securities for both retail and institutional clients, through a stock exchange or over the counter, in return for a fee or commission. Stockbrokers are known by numerous professional designations, depending on the license they hold, the type of securities they sell, or the services they provide.

7. Money market: a sector of the capital market where short-term obligations such

as treasury bills, commercial paper and bankers' acceptances are bought and sold.

8. Dividend: payments made by a corporation to its shareholder members. It is the portion of corporate profits paid out to stockholders. When a corporation earns a profit or surplus, that money can be put to two uses: it can either be re-invested in the business (called retained earnings), or it can be distributed to shareholders.

Exercises

I. Translate the following sentence into Chinese.

1. The stock market is driven solely by supply and demand. The number of shares of stock available for sale dictates the supply and the number of shares that investors want to buy dictates the demand. It's important to understand that for every share that is purchased, there is someone on the other end selling that share (or vice versa).

2. The purpose of a stock market is to facilitate the exchange of securities between buyers and sellers, reducing the risks of investing. Just imagine how difficult it would be to sell shares if you had to call around the neighborhood trying to find a buyer. Really, a stock market is nothing more than a super-sophisticated farmers' market linking buyers and sellers.

3. The NYSE is the first type of exchange (as we referred to above), where much of the trading is done face-to-face on trading floor. This is also referred to as a listed exchange. Orders come in through brokerage firms that are members of the exchange and flow down to floor brokers who go to a specific spot on the floor where the stock trades.

4. The second type of exchange is the virtual sort called an over-the-counter (OTC) market, of which the NASDAQ is the most popular. These markets have no central location or floor brokers whatsoever. Trading is done through a computer and telecommunications network of dealers.

II. Read the text and answer the following questions.

1. What is a share of stock?
2. What is a stock exchange?
3. What is the difference between primary market and secondary market?
4. What does 「over the counter」 mean?

III. Read the text and discuss.

In your opinion, why do many people consider that stock exchanges play an important role in the stock market?

Restoring Faith in the Stock Market Essential to Economy

By Huang Tiantian (China Daily)

The stock market should be a place to realize the Chinese dream and accumulate wealth by sharing in the nation's development, said economist Liu Jipeng.

As for a long-time champion for capital market reform, Liu said he is encouraged by the recent promise by Xiao Gang, the newly appointed chairman of the China Securities Regulatory Commission, that the stock market exists to serve the aspirations of the population - a political slogan emphasized by President Xi Jinping.

But effective reforms must be carried out by the commission, Liu said, to help entrepreneurs and good companies achieve their goals and generate healthy returns for their investors.

At least, the capital market should not be, as small shareholders complain, a place to kill people's dream. Some Internet reviews even went so far as to say the Chinese stock market is not a place for the Chinese dream but one for a Chinese nightmare.

It is considered by many to be absurd that China's stock market, while serving the second largest economy in the world, has performed poorly in recent years, he argued.

The stock market has failed to yield much of a return for many investors for the last five years, even though the Chinese economy came out almost unscathed in the financial crisis in 2008 and 2009 in the West and continued to lead global economic growth.

A root cause is the market's poor regulation, its rules and practices that dampen competition rather than reward competitors and favor special interests to manipulate share prices rather than protect investors, especially small shareholders.

China's stock market is therefore at a crossroads. With the National People's Congress elected in March, a new government and a new chairman were appointed to head the China Securities Regulatory Commission so 「it is high time for a change」, Liu said.

China's stock market reform can also render timely support to the central government on the macroeconomic level, argued Liu, who is a frequent commentator on China's stock market policies and also director of the capital research center of the China University of Political Science and Law.

Given the effective ban on IPOs since the middle of last year and with hundreds of companies waiting in line to get approval for a new issue of shares, the Chinese stock market is not fully functional at present.

Companies have to resort to banks and other money lenders when they need to refinance themselves, exerting an enormous demand for an increase in credit supply. But, almost inevitably, too much and too fast an increase in money supply leads to inflation.

Letting some companies, especially the more competitive ones, raise capital from the stock market can help the economy avoid such a helpless reliance on credit for reinvestment. So a robust stock market can help the government control the overall size of money, Liu said.

There is also the likelihood that it can generate money for individual investors to launch small business ventures.

It does not require rocket science to figure out how to re-boot the Chinese stock market, he added. One or two new rules, so long as they are competition-friendly, will help the commission rebuild investor confidence.

One thing that can produce an almost immediate effect is to set a limit on the percentage of all equity shares that the majority shareholder, usually a single entity in China, may hold when a company applies for commission approval for listing. 「Say 33 percent,」 he said. 「Or any figure below 40 percent.」

Other countries may not need such a limit. But it is necessary in China because many companies either have a background in government or are under the de facto control of one family.

A second need is for the commission to set a limit on the majority shareholder's selling of stock. It must be a long process – to guarantee the majority shareholder's commitment to the company, accompanied by strict information disclosure – and it must meet a pre-determined target selling price.

This proposed new rule can prevent the majority shareholder from selling its holdings immediately after its initial public offering to make money while driving down the share price and hurting other investors.

Any thing done to prevent the majority shareholder from using the public capital market to generate personal money rather than helping the company will help the commission to restore investors' respect and their confidence in the market.

「It is not a matter of money, which China has no shortage of,」Liu said.「Rather, it is to curb vested interests and a matter of political responsibility. And the CSRC must demonstrate a sense of urgency.」

New Words and Expressions

accumulate	v. 堆積，累積，逐漸增加
aspiration	n. 強烈的願望
slogan	n. 口號，標語
entrepreneur	n. 企業家，主辦人
absurd	adj. 荒謬的，荒唐的，無理性的
yield	v. 生利，獲利
unscathed	adj. 未受損傷的，未受傷害的
dampen	v. 使……沮喪，抑制
render	v. 提出，開出
resort	v. 求助於
robust	adj. 強勁的，強健的
rocket science	高深的事，難做的事
Initial Public Offering	首次公開發行

Notes

1. China Securities Regulatory Commission (CSRC): an institution of the State Council of the People's Republic of China (PRC), with ministry-level rank. It is the main regulator of the securities industry in China.

2. Financial crisis: it is applied broadly to a variety of situations in which some financial assets suddenly lose a large part of their nominal value. In the 19th and early 20th centuries, many financial crises were associated with banking panics, and many recessions coincided with these panics.

3. IPO: a type of public offering where shares of stock in a company are sold to the general public, on a securities exchange, for the first time. Through this process, a private company transforms into a public company. Initial public offerings are used by

companies to raise expansion capital, to possibly monetize the investments of early private investors, and to become publicly traded enterprises.

4. Shareholder: an individual or institution (including a corporation) that legally owns a share of stock in a public or private corporation. Stockholders are granted special privileges depending on the class of stock.

5. Capital market: a financial market for the buying and selling of long-term debt- or equity-backed securities. These markets channel the wealth of savers to those who can put it to long-term productive use, such as companies or governments making long-term investments.

6. Vested interest: it means a personal or private reason for wanting something to be done or to happen.

Exercises

I. Choose the best answer to the following questions.

1. The main reason for the stock market's existence is to satisfy _____.
   A. government's profit
   B. companies' benefit
   C. common people's demand
   D. stock exchange's interest

2. That China's stock market needs to change is not because of _____.
   A. generating healthy returns for firms' investors
   B. political responsibility
   C. China's having no shortage of money
   D. none of the above

II. Read the text and answer the following questions.

1. Why has the stock market failed to yield much of a return for many investors for the last five years?

2. Why does Liu consider that the commission should set a limit on the majority shareholder's selling of stock?

III. Translate the article into Chinese.

Why Invest Money in the Stock Market

Perhaps you can guess what happens at a stock market from its name. It is called a market because it is a place where some people sell things and others buy things. An exchange of things takes place. The things that are exchanged at the stock market are shares of stock in businesses or companies. The shares represent a partial ownership of the company. In other words, if you buy shares of stock in a business, you become a partial owner of the business. The stock market or stock exchange, then, is a place where people can buy or sell shares in a particular company or business.

Why does a company want to share its money with other people? There are several reasons: First, the company may be doing very well. It may need money to expand. By selling shares of stock, the company can get the money it needs. Sometimes, it is advantageous for the company to 「go public」 for tax reasons. Because of the tax laws, the company may save money on taxes by selling shares on the stock exchange. Sometimes, a company may owe a lot of money to banks. By selling shares of stock, it may be able to pay the banks. Many companies sell stock for this reason. However, the reasons why companies sell their stock on the stock exchange are often complex. In general, all companies that sell shares of stock on the stock exchange need to raise money for one reason or another.

Reading Comprehension

Special Financial Instruments

Financial derivatives are financial instruments whose value is derived from the value of something else. They generally take the form of contracts under which the parties agree to payments between them based upon the value of an underlying asset or other date at a particular point in time. The main types of derivatives are futures, options, forwards and swaps.

The main use of derivatives is to reduce risk for one party while offering the potential for a high return (at increased risk) to another. The diverse range of potential underlying assets and pay off alternatives leads to a huge range of derivatives contracts available to be traded in the market. Derivatives can be based on different types of assets such as commodities, equities (stocks), bonds, interest rates, exchange rates, or indexes. Their performance can determine both the amount and the timing of the payoffs.

One use of derivatives is as a tool to transfer risk by taking an equal but opposite position in the futures market against the underlying commodity. For example, a farmer will buy/sell futures contracts on a crop from/to a speculator before the harvest since the farmer intends to eventually sell his crop after the harvest. By taking a position in the futures market, the farmer minimizes his risk from price fluctuations.

Of course, speculators may trade with other speculators as well as with hedgers. In most financial derivatives markets, the value of speculative trading is far higher than the value of true hedge trading. As well as outright speculation, derivatives traders may also look for arbitrage opportunities between different derivatives on identical or closely related underlying securities. Derivatives such as options, futures or swaps, generally offer the greatest possible reward for betting on whether the price of an underlying asset will go up or down. For example, a person may believe that a drug company may find a cure for cancer in the next year. If the person bought the stock for $10.00, and it went to $20.00 after the cure was announced, the person would have made a 100% profit and have a return of 100%. If he borrowed money to buy the stock in US (in US law the general maximum he could borrow would be $5.00 or half the purchase price), he would have used only $5.00 of his own money and thus made a 100% profit with a return of 300%. However, if he paid a 1 dollar option premium to buy the stock at 11 dollars, when it shot up to 20 dollars he could have received the difference (9 dollars) and thus made an 800% profit and a return of 800%.

Other uses of derivatives are to gain an economic exposure to an underlying security in situations where direct ownership of the underlying is too costly or is prohibited by legal or regulatory restrictions, or to create a synthetic short position. In addition to directional plays (i.e. simply betting on the direction of the underlying security), speculators can use derivatives to place bets on the volatility of the underlying security. This technique is commonly used when speculating with traded options. Speculative trading in derivatives gained a great deal of notoriety in 1995 when Nick Leeson, a trader at Barings Bank, made poor and unauthorized investments in index futures. Through a combination of poor judgment on his part, lack of oversight by management, a naive regulatory environment and unfortunate outside events like the Kobe earthquake, Leeson incurred a $1.4 billion loss that bankrupted the centuries-old financial institution.

The derivatives market serves the needs of several groups of users, including those parties such as the hedger who enters the market to reduce risk. Hedging usually involves taking a position in a derivative financial instrument, which has opposite return characteristics of the item being hedged, to offset losses or gains; the speculator who enters the derivatives market in search of profits, is willing to accept risk. A speculator takes an open position in a derivative product and the arbitrageur who is a speculator attempts to lock in near riskless profit from price differences by simultaneously entering into the purchase and sale of substantially identical financial instruments. Other participants include clearing houses or clearing corporations, brokers, commodity futures trading commission, commodity pool operators, commodity trading advisors, financial institutions and banks, futures exchange, and futures commission merchants.

In the financial market, the familiar derivative instruments are classified as: Forward Contracts, Futures Contracts, Options and Swaps. Derivatives can also be classified as either forward-based (e.g., futures, forward contracts, and swap contracts), option-based (e.g., call or put option), or combinations of the two. A forward-based contract obligates one party to buy and a counter party to sell an underlying asset, such as foreign currency or a commodity, with equal risk at a future date at an agreed-on price. Option-based contracts (e.g., call options, put options, caps and floors) provide the holder with a right, but not an obligation to buy or sell an underlying financial instrument, foreign currency, or commodity at an agreed-on price during a specified time period or at a specified date.

New Words and Expressions

derivatives	*n.*	金融衍生品
instrument	*n.*	工具
speculator	*n.*	投機商
equity	*adj.*	股票的，股市的
hedger	*n.*	作套期保值的人
futures	*n.*	期貨
options	*n.*	期權
swap	*n.*	掉期
underlying asset		基礎資產
premium	*n.*	保證金
short position		空頭，短缺頭寸

bankrupt	vt.	使破產，使枯竭
offset	vt.	抵消；補償
clearinghouse	n.	票據交換所
commission	n.	佣金，手續費

Notes

1. Futures: a financial contract that encompasses the sale of financial instruments or physical commodities for future delivery, usually on a commodity exchange. Futures contracts try to 「bet」 what the value of an index or commodity will be at some date in the future.

2. Futures contracts: an agreement to purchase or sell a commodity for delivery in the future: (1) at a price that is determined at initiation of the contract; (2) which obligates each party to the contract to fulfill the contract at the specified price; (3) which is used to assume or shift price risk; and (4) which may be satisfied by delivery or offset.

3. Delivery: the transfer of the cash commodity from the seller of a futures contract to the buyer of a futures contract. Each futures exchange has specific procedures for delivery of a cash commodity. Some futures contracts, such as stock index contracts, are cash settled.

4. Financial instrument: there are two basic types: (1) a debt instrument, which is a loan with an agreement to pay back funds with interest; (2) an equity security, which is a share or stock in a company.

5. Underlying: a specified interest rate, security price, commodity price, foreign exchange rate, index of prices or rates, or other variable (including the occurrence or nonoccurrence of a specified event such as a scheduled payment under a contract). An underlying may be a price or rate of an asset or liability but is not the asset or liability itself.

6. Forward contracts: a cash transaction common in many industries, including commodity merchandising, in which a commercial buyer and seller agree upon delivery of a specified quality and quantity of goods at a specified future date. A price may be agreed upon in advance, or there may be agreement that the price will be determined at the time of delivery.

7. Futures market: an auction market in which participants buy and sell commodity/future contracts for delivery on a specified future date. Trading is carried out through open yelling and hand signals in a trading pit.

8. Short position: the practice of selling securities or other financial instruments that are not currently owned, with the intention of subsequently repurchasing them (「covering」) at a lower price.

9. Swaps: a derivative in which counterparties exchange cash flows of one party's financial instrument for those of the other party's financial instrument. The benefits in question depend on the type of financial instruments involved.

Exercises

I. Choose the best answer to the following questions.

1. Which of the following are among underlying assets of financial derivatives?
    A. Commodities.
    B. Bonds and stocks.
    C. Exchange rate, interest rate and indices.
    D. All of the above.

2. Which of the following statements is not true about derivatives traders?
    A. They look for arbitrage opportunities between different derivatives.
    B. They are farmers who sell their crops before harvest.
    C. They use derivatives as a tool to transfer risk of price volatility of the underlying assets.
    D. They use derivatives to place bets on the volatility of the underlying security.

3. How many groups are derivative contracts divided into according to the way they are traded in the market?
    A. Two.   B. Three.
    C. Four.   D. Not mentioned.

II. Translate the following sentences into Chinese.

1. In most financial derivatives markets, the value of speculative trading is far higher than the value of true hedge trading. As well as outright speculation, derivatives traders may also look for arbitrage opportunities between different derivatives on identical or closely related underlying securities. Derivatives such as options, futures or swaps, generally offer the greatest possible reward for betting on whether the price of

an underlying asset will go up or down.

2. The derivatives market serves the needs of several groups of users, including those parties such as the hedger who enters the market to reduce risk. Hedging usually involves taking a position in a derivative financial instrument, which has opposite return characteristics of the item being hedged, to offset losses or gains.

III. Read the text and answer the following questions.

1. What are the derivatives in the financial market?
2. What are the functions of derivatives based on the text?
3. According to the text, how many types of derivative instruments are there?

Part Three   Investment Risk Management

Who Is to Blame for the Subprime Crisis?

By Eric Petroff

Anytime something bad happens, it doesn't take long before blame starts to be assigned. In the instance of subprime mortgage woes, there is no single entity or individual to point the finger at. Instead, this mess is a collective creation of the world's central banks, homeowners, lenders, credit rating agencies and underwriters, and investors. Let's investigate.

The Mess

The economy was at risk of a deep recession after the dotcom bubble burst in early 2000; this situation was compounded by the September 11 terrorist attacks that followed in 2001. In response, central banks around the world tried to stimulate the economy. They created capital liquidity through a reduction in interest rates. In turn, investors sought higher returns through riskier investments. Lenders took on greater risks too, and approved subprime mortgage loans to borrowers with poor credit. Consumer demand drove the housing bubble to all-time highs in the summer of 2005, which ultimately collapsed in August of 2006.

The end result of these key events was increased foreclosure activity, large lenders and hedge funds declaring bankruptcy, and fears regarding further decreases in economic growth and consumer spending. So who's to blame? Let's take a look at the key players.

Biggest Culprit: The Lenders

Most of the blame should be pointed at the mortgage originators (lenders) for creating these problems. It was the lenders who ultimately lent funds to people with poor credit and a high risk of default.

When the central banks flooded the markets with capital liquidity, it not only lowered interest rates, it also broadly depressed risk premiums as investors sought riskier opportunities to bolster their investment returns. At the same time, lenders found themselves with ample capital to lend and, like investors, an increased willingness to undertake additional risk to increase their investment returns.

In defense of the lenders, there was an increased demand for mortgages, and housing prices were increasing because interest rates had dropped substantially. At the time, lenders probably saw subprime mortgages as less of a risk than they really were: rates were low, the economy was healthy and people were making their payments.

As you can see in Figure 1, subprime mortgage originations grew from $173 billion in 2001 to a record level of $665 billion in 2005, which represented an increase of nearly 300%. There is a clear relationship between the liquidity following September 11, 2001, and subprime loan originations; lenders were clearly willing and able to provide borrowers with the necessary funds to purchase a home.

Subprime Mortgage Originations

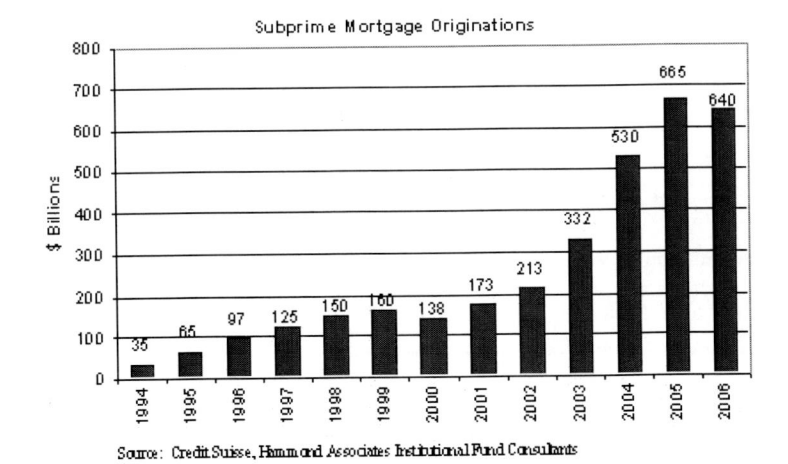

Year	$ Billions
1994	35
1995	65
1996	97
1997	125
1998	150
1999	160
2000	138
2001	173
2002	213
2003	332
2004	530
2005	665
2006	640

Source: Credit Suisse, Hammond Associates Institutional Fund Consultants

Figure 1

Note: The data presented herein are believed to be reliable but have not been independently verified. Any such information may be incomplete or condensed.

Partner In Crime: Home buyers

While we're on the topic of lenders, we should also mention the home buyers. Many were playing an extremely risky game by buying houses they could barely afford. They were able to make these purchases with non-traditional mortgages (such as 2/28 and interest-only mortgages) that offered low introductory rates and minimal initial costs such as「no down payment」. Their hope lay in price appreciation, which would have allowed them to refinance at lower rates and take the equity out of the home for use in other spending. However, instead of continued appreciation, the housing bubble burst, and prices dropped rapidly.

As a result, when their mortgages reset, many homeowners were unable to refinance their mortgages to lower rates, as there was no equity being created as housing prices fell. They were, therefore, forced to reset their mortgage at higher rates, which many could not afford. Many homeowners were simply forced to default on their mortgages. Foreclosures continued to increase through 2006 and 2007.

In their exuberance to hook more subprime borrowers, some lenders or mortgage brokers may have given the impression that there was no risk to these mortgages and that the costs weren't that high; however, at the end of the day, many borrowers simply assumed mortgages they couldn't reasonably afford. Had they not made such an aggressive purchase and assumed a less risky mortgage, the overall effects might have been manageable.

Exacerbating the situation, lenders and investors of securities backed by these defaulting mortgages suffered. Lenders lost money on defaulted mortgages as they were increasingly left with property that was worth less than the amount originally loaned. In many cases, the losses were large enough to result in bankruptcy.

Investment Banks Worsen the Situation

The increased use of the secondary mortgage market by lenders added to the number of subprime loans lenders could originate. Instead of holding the originated mortgages on their books, lenders were able to simply sell off the mortgages in the secondary market and collect the originating fees. This freed up more capital for even more lending, which increased liquidity even more. The snowball began to build momentum.

A lot of the demand for these mortgages came from the creation of assets that pooled mortgages together into a security, such as a collateralized debt obligation

(CDO). In this process, investment banks would buy the mortgages from lenders and securitize these mortgages into bonds, which were sold to investors through CDOs.

Rating Agencies: Possible Conflict of Interest

A lot of criticism has been directed at the rating agencies and underwriters of the CDOs and other mortgage-backed securities that included subprime loans in their mortgage pools. Some argue that the rating agencies should have foreseen the high default rates for subprime borrowers, and they should have given these CDOs much lower ratings than the 「AAA」 rating given to the higher quality tranches. If the ratings had been more accurate, fewer investors would have bought into these securities, and the losses may not have been as bad.

Moreover, some have pointed to the conflict of interest between rating agencies, which receive fees from a security's creator, and their ability to give an unbiased assessment of risk. The argument is that rating agencies were enticed to give better ratings in order to continue receiving service fees, or they run the risk of the underwriter going to a different rating agency (or the security not getting rated at all). However, on the flip side, it's hard to sell a security if it is not rated. Regardless of the criticism surrounding the relationship between underwriters and rating agencies, the fact of the matter is that they were simply bringing bonds to market based on market demand.

Fuel to the Fire: Investor Behavior

Just as the homeowners are to blame for their purchases gone wrong, much of the blame also must be placed on those who invested in CDOs. Investors were the ones willing to purchase these CDOs at ridiculously low premiums over Treasury bonds. These enticingly low rates are what ultimately led to such huge demand for subprime loans.

Much of the blame here lies with investors because it is up to individuals to perform due diligence on their investments and make appropriate expectations. Investors failed in this by taking the 「AAA」 CDO ratings at face value.

Final Culprit: Hedge Funds

Another party that added to the mess was the hedge fund industry. It aggravated the problem not only by pushing rates lower, but also by fueling the market volatility that caused investor losses. The failures of a few investment managers also contributed to the problem.

To illustrate, there is a type of hedge fund strategy that can be best described as 「credit arbitrage」. It involves purchasing subprime bonds on credit and hedging these positions with credit default swaps. This amplified demand for CDOs; by using leverage, a fund could purchase a lot more CDOs and bonds than it could with existing capital alone, pushing subprime interest rates lower and further fueling the problem. Moreover, because leverage was involved, this set the stage for a spike in volatility, which is exactly what happened as soon as investors realized the true, lesser quality of subprime CDOs.

Because hedge funds use a significant amount of leverage, losses were amplified and many hedge funds shut down operations as they ran out of money in the face of margin calls. (For more on this, see Massive Hedge Fund Failures and Losing The Amaranth Gamble.)

Plenty of Blame to Go Around

Overall, it was a mix of factors and participants that precipitated the current subprime mess. Ultimately, though, human behavior and greed drove the demand, supply and the investor appetite for these types of loans. Hindsight is always 20/20, and it is now obvious that there was a lack of wisdom on the part of many. However, there are countless examples of markets lacking wisdom, most recently the dotcom bubble and ensuing 「irrational exuberance」 on the part of investors. It seems to be a fact of life that investors will always extrapolate current conditions too far into the future – good, bad or ugly. For a one-stop shop on subprime mortgages and the subprime meltdown, check out the Subprime Mortgages Feature.

New Words and Expressions

subprime	*adj.*	準最低貸款利率的
mess	*n.*	混亂；困境；骯髒
underwriter	*n.*	保險業者；保險公司；承諾支付者；擔保人
recession	*n.*	經濟衰退，不景氣
Dot-com	*n.*	網路公司
liquidity	*n.*	流動性；流動資金
foreclosure	*n.*	喪失抵押品贖回權
culprit	*n.*	犯人，肇事者，被告人

premium	n.	保險費；額外費用
mortgage	n.	抵押；抵押單據，抵押證明
refinance	v.	再為……籌錢；對……再供資金
exacerbate	vt.	激怒；使惡化
default	vi.	未履行任務或責任；拖欠
criticism	n.	批評，批判；鑒定
arbitrage	n.	仲裁；套匯，套利
irrational	adj.	無理性的；不合理的
exuberance	n.	繁茂，豐富；充沛
extrapolate	v.	（由已知資料對未知事實或價值）推算，推斷

Notes

1. Subprime mortgage crisis: It was a nationwide banking emergency that coincided with the U. S. recession of December 2007 – June 2009. It was triggered by a large decline in home prices after the collapse of a housing bubble, leading to mortgage delinquencies and foreclosures and the devaluation of housing – related securities.

2. Credit rating agency: (CRA, also called a ratings service) is a company that assigns credit ratings, which rate a debtor's ability to pay back debt by making timely interest payments and the likelihood of default. An agency may rate the creditworthiness of issuers of debt obligations, of debt instruments, [1] and in some cases, of the servicers of the underlying debt, [2] but not of individual consumers.

3. Dot – com bubble: It was a historic speculative bubble covering roughly 1997 – 2000 (with a climax on March 10, 2000, with the NASDAQ peaking at 5, 132. 52 in intraday trading before closing at 5, 048. 62) during which stock markets in industrialized nations saw their equity value rise rapidly from growth in the Internet sector and related fields.

4. Hedge fund: It is an investment fund that pools capital from a limited number of accredited individual or institutional investors and invests in a variety of assets, often with complex portfolio construction and risk management techniques.

5. down payment: or (downpayment) is a payment used in the context of the purchase of expensive items such as a car and a house, whereby the payment is the initial upfront portion of the total amount due and it is usually given in cash at the time of

finalizing the transaction. [1] A loan or the amount in cash is then required to make the full payment.

6. Collateralized debt obligation : (CDO) is a type of structured asset-backed security (ABS). Originally developed for the corporate debt markets, over time CDOs evolved to encompass the mortgage and mortgage-backed security (「MBS」) markets.

7. due diligence : It is an investigation of a business or person prior to signing a contract, or an act with a certain standard of care. It can be a legal obligation, but the term will more commonly apply to voluntary investigations.

Exercises

I. Choose the best answer to the following questions.

1. During the housing prices were increasing because _____.
    A. People can gain more salary
    B. The interest rate of loan decreased gradually
    C. Central bank can offer more money
    D. The demand of houses increased

2. The main criticism of rating agencies is _____
    A. they had seen the default rates for subprime borrowers.
    B. they have given these CDOs much lower ratings than the 「AAA」 rating.
    C. they have given these CDOs higher ratings than the 「AA」 rating.
    D. they should do not give any opinion on these CDOs.

II. Translate the following sentences into Chinese.

1. Central banks around the world tried to stimulate the economy. They created capital liquidity through a reduction in interest rates. In turn, investors sought higher returns through riskier investments. Lenders took on greater risks too, and approved subprime mortgage loans to borrowers with poor credit. Consumer demand drove the housing bubble to all-time highs in the summer of 2005, which ultimately collapsed in August of 2006.

2. Exacerbating the situation, lenders and investors of securities backed by these defaulting mortgages suffered. Lenders lost money on defaulted mortgages as they were increasingly left with property that was worth less than the amount originally loaned. In many cases, the losses were large enough to result in bankruptcy.

3. The argument is that rating agencies were enticed to give better ratings in order to continue receiving service fees, or they run the risk of the underwriter going to a different rating agency. However, on the flip side, it's hard to sell a security if it is not rated. Regardless of the criticism surrounding the relationship between underwriters and rating agencies, the fact of the matter is that they were simply bringing bonds to market based on market demand.

III. Read the text and answer the following questions.

1. In this article, why the writer said most of the blame should be pointed at the mortgage
    originators for creating subprime problems?
2. Why the investment Banks worsen this financial crisis?
3. What does credit arbitrage mean?

Chapter Four: Insurance

Part One Insurance

Reading Comprehension

Filling China's Insurance Gaps

By Diao Ying (China Daily)

China is home to some of the largest insurers in the world, but with the industry still at a nascent stage, huge opportunities remain. While premium income from insurance was 1.43 trillion yuan ($230 million; 180 billion euros) last year and total assets of the industry were 5 trillion yuan, there remain major gaps in coverage.

Specialized areas including agriculture and disaster insurance have yet to take off. And extreme niches found in developed markets are unheard of. Now specialist insurers from the West are on the way to fill the gaps, looking to profit from China's growth by providing their experience and expertise.

Lloyd's, the world's largest specialist insurer is among them. It aims to increase its China business faster than the country's GDP growth in the coming years, says the company's chairman, John Nelson. It also plans to develop Shanghai into one of its international centers for insurance and reinsurance.

Opportunities for foreign insurers have emerged as a result of China's fast-growing economy. This is particularly true of less developed areas of the country and industries more prone to natural disasters, such as agriculture. The China Insurance Regulatory Commission, the nation's insurance regulator, said in July that it will speed up efforts to improve insurance coverage for agriculture and disasters.

Insurance is one of Britain's largest industries, employing 350,000 people,

50,000 in London alone, and contributing 2.5 percent of the country's GDP. In China, by comparison, insurance is largely underdeveloped, but is growing rapidly. According to the 12th Five-Year Plan (2011-2015), China's insurance industry premium income is set to reach 3 trillion yuan and the industry's total assets 10 trillion yuan by 2015.

Lloyd's has its roots in Edward Lloyd's coffee house in London where ship owners met to make insurance deals 300 years ago. Since then it has insured property and personal wealth against war, disaster and accidents. Among its most notable insurance deals was the ill-fated Titanic. The company's China footprint is fairly recent. Lloyd's opened its first China office in Shanghai in 2007 and received a license to provide direct insurance in the country last year.

Lloyd's business model is new to China. In a world where most business is conducted electronically, it provides a market where insurers and brokers meet face-to-face, in an atmosphere of both cooperation and competition. Around the company's London headquarters, men and women in dark business suits carrying thick files abound, flitting between deals to insure anything from oil rigs to celebrity body parts.

Its biggest strength in China, says Richard Ward, chief executive, is that it can insure complex risks that other players do not know how to. 「If you want to insure a satellite launch, we know how to do that; if you want to insure property against earthquake risk, we know how to do that. We are not going to compete with the People's Insurance Company of China in the local market for motor insurance, or China Pacific Insurance Group for property,」 says Ward. 「We are competing for the more complex risks when you need special skills.」 The growth potential of the Chinese insurance market is both attractive and challenging, he says. 「The market in China is highly competitive, to the extent that we worry about the profitability of business,」 he says.

Nelson says moving too fast in a developing market can be dangerous. 「It is better to write no business than to write unprofitable business. That is the message we are giving our team in China,」 he says.

Under the Lloyd's structure, insurers form syndicates to sign contracts. According to this model, the key in China is to build relationships with local insurers and let them push the business.

Lloyd's has hired Eric Gao, who previously worked for Swiss Re, to lead its China operations, with about 25 people working under him. 「It is a matter of having people on the ground, leaving their office and meeting the local business community,」says Ward.

In addition to the domestic market, insurers could also profit from Chinese companies operating overseas. For example, China Ocean Shipping Company is increasing the number of vessels it has around the world and needs to insure them. Similarly, the aviation industry operates globally and needs overseas insurance. This will create opportunities for specialist insurers, Ward says.

However, there are issues for international insurers looking to expand in China. Above all, Chinese people differ from Westerners in their attitude to risks. Chinese companies are better known for hard work than taking risk.

「It will take a while for Lloyd's to understand China in the way it understands other markets and vice versa,」says Nelson.

Regulatory and judicial systems in China are still developing and could also be a barrier. In the UK, the judicial system is highly developed and trustworthy. This is a precondition for Lloyd's operations.

「In order for the Chinese insurance market to develop, China needs to develop the same kind of reputation,」says Ward.

Lloyd's business model also faces potential domestic challenges. For example, Shanghai is considering opening its own insurance exchange. 「We all compete with each other,」says Ward. 「But it is difficult to replicate a market. It is not something you build from scratch.」

With more communication on both sides, things may improve. Chinese insurers are sending people to the West to learn about business practice. China Reinsurance Corp, the largest reinsurer in China, last year joined Lloyd's and became the first Chinese member of the market. It put $50 million into a syndicate along with Catlin, the biggest insurer in the market.

Lloyd's also wants to increase the number of Chinese nationals working in London. At the junior levels, it plans to hire from China's large student population in the UK through its graduate program. It also plans to send staff from Shanghai to London. The intention is that these Chinese nationals take their experience of China to London, and then return to China with a better understanding of the global insurance market.

「Creating business footprints both ways will create more connections and more business,」says Nelson.

This year China resent six people to work in London. Steven Catlin, chairman of Catlin Group Limited, says it also sends its people to work at the sites of Chinese insurers to learn about how they do business. Catlin opened its second China office in Beijing this year, following an earlier one in Shanghai.

「As the Chinese economy develops, and as the Chinese insurance companies become more sensitive to their own internal capital, there will be a healthier market in which we can operate,」says Nelson.

New Words and Expressions

nascent	*adj.*	初期的；初生的；開始形成的
premium	*n.*	保險費
coverage	*n.*	範圍，保險項目
insurer	*n.*	保險人
reinsurance	*n.*	再保險
China Insurance Regulatory Commission		保監會
trillion	*n.*	萬億；兆
Lloyd's	*n.*	［英］勞埃德海上保險協會，勞埃德商船協會
aviation	*n.*	航空；飛機製造業
judicial system		法院系統
insurance exchange		保險交易所

Notes

1. Insurance rate: the percentage relationship between the insurance premium and the coverage it buys.

2. Health insurance: insurance against loss by illness or bodily injury. Health insurance provides coverage for medical expense. Policies differ in what they cover, the size of the deductible and/or co-payment, limits of coverage and the options for treatment available to the policyholder.

3. Reinsurance: insurance that is purchased by an insurance company from one or more other insurance companies (the「reinsurer」) as a means of risk management. The ceding company and the reinsurer enter into a reinsurance agreement which details

the conditions upon which the reinsurer would pay a share of the claims incurred by the ceding company. The reinsurer is paid a 「reinsurance premium」 by the ceding company, which issues insurance policies to its own policyholders.

4. China Insurance Regulatory Commission (CIRC): an agency of China authorized by the State Council to regulate the Chinese insurance products and services market and maintain legal and stable operations of insurance industry. It was founded on November 18, 1998, upgraded from a semi-ministerial to a ministerial institution in 2003, and currently has 31 local offices in every province.

5. Lloyd's: also called Lloyd's of London, is a British insurance and reinsurance market, known as underwriters, or 「members」, both individuals (traditionally known as 「names」) and corporations, come together to pool and spread risk. Unlike most of its competitors in the industry, it is not a company but it is a corporate body governed by the Lloyd's Act 1871 and subsequent Acts of the Parliament of the United Kingdom.

Exercises

I. Choose the best answer to the following questions.

1. Based on the text, in the insurance industry, which do specialized areas include?

  A. Property.　　　　　　　　B. Life.
  C. Auto.　　　　　　　　　　D. Agriculture.

2. Lloyd's business model exclude _____.
  A. insurers and brokers meet each other
  B. there is a cooperation between insurers and brokers
  C. there is a competition between insurers and brokers
  D. insurers and brokers can wear informal dresses

3. Lloyd's can insure complex risks that include _____.
  A. fire risk　　　　　　　　　B. satellite launch risk
  C. earthquake risk　　　　　　D. Both B and C

II. Translate the following sentences into Chinese.

1. Opportunities for foreign insurers have emerged as a result of China's fast-growing economy. This is particularly true of less developed areas of the country and industries more prone to natural disasters, such as agriculture. The China Insurance Regula-

tory Commission, the nation's insurance regulator, said in July that it will speed up efforts to improve insurance coverage for agriculture and disasters.

2. With more communication on both sides, things may improve. Chinese insurers are sending people to the West to learn about business practice. China Reinsurance Corp, the largest reinsurer in China, last year joined Lloyd's and became the first Chinese member of the market. It put $50 million into a syndicate along with Catlin, the biggest insurer in the market.

3. As the Chinese economy develops, and as the Chinese insurance companies become more sensitive to their own internal capital, there will be a healthier market in which we can operate.

III. Read the text and answer the following questions.

1. Why do foreign insurance firms want to come into Chinese insurance market?
2. What is the Lloyd's development goals in China?
3. What is the Lloyd's advantages when it faces Chinese customers?

Part Two   Life Insurance

Reading Comprehension

Secure Future for Life Insurance

By Yu Ran in Shanghai (China Daily)

China is expected to be the world's second-largest life insurance market by 2020, having a total gross premiums of $406 billion, according to statistics released by McKinsey & Company on Tuesday.

The scale of the life insurance market in China, which will take the No. 2 spot from Japan, will be doubled and it will see an annual growth of 10 percent in the coming five to 10 years. A new edition of the book *Life Insurance in Asia*, written by two senior McKinsey partners, pointed out that as a newly booming market with potential profits for life insurance users, market capitalization in its life insurance market is growing by about 15 percent every year, which is still a long way behind developed economies.

「China's rising middle class, of which there are expected to be 500 million by 2025, has been gradually shifting financial assets from low-paying deposits into higher-yielding investments, creating new opportunities for the insurance sector,」said Stephan Binder, a senior partner and head of McKinsey's insurance practice in the Asia-Pacific region, and one of the authors of the book.

Binder added that demand for insurance in China will contribute an estimated 25 percent to insurance growth globally over the next five years. Middle-class families are expected to be the major group of life insurance customers in China. 「By 2015, the middle-class group in both first-tier and second- or third-tier cities will represent 30 percent of the urban population, contributing more than 30 percent to the growth of the life insurance market,」said Binder. For middle-class parents, buying life insurance has become an essential step especially when a new family member is born.

「My parents bought life insurance for me when I was 18 years old, and I got my daughter education insurance, investment insurance and life insurance when she was two months old,」said Hu Cong, the 28-year-old mother of a 2-year-old girl from Wenzhou, Zhejiang Province.

According to the book, bancassurance has grown the fastest in the past decade by challenging the traditional tied agency model in China.

「It's hard for insurance agents to provide long-term attractive life insurance products with investment profits for local customers, who had been persuaded by their financial managers to buy insurance products through banks,」said Parker Shi, a senior leader of McKinsey's insurance practice.

Shi added that cooperation between the insurance companies and banks is encouraged. At the moment, insurance companies are competing with banks as suppliers of insurance products for limited profits. 「It turned out to be very difficult to find new clients to buy life insurance in the past two to three years while banks launched certain insurance-related products with profitable returns,」said Wang Huanhuan, a sales manager of a local insurance company in Shanghai.

Wang added that the company will probably work with a number of banks to launch several life insurance products in the near future. In addition, in China's highly competitive insurance market, foreign companies are finding it hard to attract customers.

The book showed that the market share of foreign insurance companies in China has continued to decline over the past five years to the current level of 5 percent.

「To succeed in China, foreign insurance firms need to follow a clear and consistent strategy that avoids the tendency to sacrifice long-term health for short-term performance,」 said Binder. He added that foreign companies arriving in China should get to know local customers better by offering appropriate personalized products and adopting a long-term strategy.

New Words and Expressions

life insurance	人身保險
annual	adj. 每年的
senior	adj. 地位較高的，資歷較深的
booming	adj. 急速發展的
capitalization	n. 資本化
bancassurance	n. [英] 銀行保險業
agency	n. 代理；機構
launch	v. 投入；著手進行；熱衷於……

Notes

1. Life insurance: a contract between an insured (insurance policy holder) and an insurer, where the insurer promises to pay a designated beneficiary a sum of money (the「benefits」) upon the death of the insured person. Depending on the contract, other events such as terminal illness or critical illness may also trigger payment.

2. The Bank Insurance Model (BIM): also sometimes known as「bancassurance」, is the partnership or relationship between a bank and an insurance company whereby the insurance company uses the bank sales channel in order to sell insurance products.

Exercises

I. Choose the best answer to the following questions.

1. Nowadays, which country is the world's second-largest life insurance market?

    A. China　　　　　　　　　　B. Japan
    C. America　　　　　　　　　D. England

2. Buying life insurance has become a vital action especially when _____.

    A. the person becomes a mother   B. children begin school

    C. a new family member is born   D. All of above

3. If foreign insurance firms want to succeed in China, they need to follow a strategy to _____.

    A. understand Chinese customers

    B. bring foreign products into China

    C. hire local people as employees

    D. introduce foreign culture to Chinese customers

II. Translate the following sentences into Chinese.

1. China's rising middle class, of which there are expected to be 500 million by 2025, has been gradually shifting financial assets from low-paying deposits into higher-yielding investments, creating new opportunities for the insurance sector.

2. Cooperation between the insurance companies and banks is encouraged. At the moment, insurance companies are competing with banks as suppliers of insurance products for limited profits. ⌈It turned out to be very difficult to find new clients to buy life insurance in the past two to three years while banks launched certain insurance-related products with profitable returns.⌋

III. Read the text and answer the following questions.

1. Why does the writer consider that middle-class families are expected to be the major group of life insurance customers in China?

2. Why did Parker Shi say ⌈it's hard for insurance agents to provide long-term attractive life insurance products with investment profits for local customers⌋?

3. What may be the reason that foreign insurance companies in China have continued to decline over the past five years?

Part Three Non-life Insurance

Reading Comprehension

Property Insurance Provides Protection Against Risks to Property

Property insurance provides protection against risks to property, such as fire, theft or weather damage. This includes specialized forms of insurance such as fire insurance, flood insurance, earthquake insurance, home insurance, inland marine insurance or boiler insurance.

Automobile insurance, known in the UK as motor insurance, is probably the most common form of insurance and may cover both legal liability claims against the driver and loss of or damage to the insured's vehicle itself. Throughout the United States an auto insurance policy is required to legally operate a motor vehicle on public roads. In some jurisdictions, bodily injury compensation for automobile accident victims has been changed to a no-fault system, which reduces or eliminates the ability to sue for compensation but provides automatic eligibility for benefits. Credit card companies insure against damage on rented cars. Driving School Insurance provides cover for any authorized driver whilst undergoing tuition cover, also unlike other motor policies provides cover for instructor liability where both the pupil and driving instructor are equally liable in the event of a claim.

Aviation insurance insures against hull, spares, deductibles, hull wear and liability risks.

Boiler insurance (also known as boiler and machinery insurance or equipment breakdown insurance) insures against accidental physical damage to equipment or machinery.

Builder's risk insurance insures against the risk of physical loss or damage to property during construction. Builder's risk insurance is typically written on an 「all risk」 basis covering damage due to any cause (including the negligence of the insured) not otherwise expressly excluded.

As for crop insurance, farmers use it to reduce or manage various risks associated with growing crops. Such risks include crop loss or damage caused by weather, hail, drought, frost damage, insects, or disease, for instance.

Earthquake insurance is a form of property insurance that pays the policyholder in the event of an earthquake that causes damage to the property. Most ordinary homeowners insurance policies feature a high deductible. Rates depend on location and the probability of an earthquake, as well as the construction of the home.

A fidelity bond is a form of casualty insurance that covers policyholders for losses that they incur as a result of fraudulent acts by specified individuals. It usually insures a business for losses caused by the dishonest acts of its employees.

Flood insurance protects against property loss due to flooding. Many insurers in the U.S. do not provide flood insurance in some portions of the country. In response to this, the federal government creates the National Flood Insurance Program which serves as the insurer of last resort.

Landlord insurance is specifically designed for people who own properties which they rent out. Most house insurance cover in the U.K will not be valid if the property is rented out. Therefore landlords must take out this specialist form of home insurance.

Marine insurance and marine cargo insurance cover the loss or damage of ships at sea or on inland waterways, and of the cargo that may be on them. When the owner of the cargo and the carrier are separate corporations, marine cargo insurance typically compensates the owner of cargo for losses sustained from fire, shipwreck, etc., but excludes losses that can be recovered from the carrier or the carrier's insurance. Many marine insurance underwriters will include 「time element」 coverage in such policies, which extends the indemnity to cover loss of profit and other business expenses attributable to the delay caused by a covered loss.

Surety bond insurance is a three-party insurance guaranteeing the performance of the principal.

Terrorism insurance provides protection against any loss or damage caused by terrorist activities.

Volcano insurance is an insurance that covers volcano damage in Hawaii.

Windstorm insurance is an insurance covering the damage that can be caused by hurricanes and tropical cyclones.

New Words and Expressions

compensation	n.	賠償，賠償金
aviation	n.	航空；飛行術，航空學
fidelity	n.	忠誠，忠實
policyholder	n.	投保人，保險客戶
instructor liability	n.	指導者，教師
hail	n.	冰雹
cargo	n.	（船或飛機裝載的）貨物；負荷
carrier	n.	承運人，運輸公司
underwriter	n.	保險業者，保險公司，保險商
indemnity	n.	賠償；保障；賠償金

Notes

1. Legal liability: is the legal bound obligation to pay debts. In law, a person is legally liable when they are financially and legally responsible for something. Legal liability concerns both civil law and criminal law. Legal liability can arise from various areas of law, such as contracts, tort judgments or settlements, taxes.

2. Policyholder: is one who pays the premium specified in the Policy Schedule to the insurance corporation.

3. Marine insurance: covers the loss or damage of ships, cargo, terminals, and any transport or cargo by which property is transferred, acquired, or held between the points of origin and final destination.

4. Cargo insurance: is a sub-branch of marine insurance, though Marine also includes Onshore and Offshore exposed property (container terminals, ports, oil platforms, pipelines), Hull, Marine Casualty, and Marine Liability.

5. Underwriter: refers to the process that a large financial service provider (bank, insurer, investment house) uses to assess the eligibility of a customer to receive their products (equity capital, insurance, mortgage, or credit).

Exercises

I. Choose the best answer to the following questions.

1. In this article, which of the following is probably the most common form of insurance?
   A. Fire insurance.
   B. Motor insurance.
   C. Flood insurance.
   D. Home insurance.

2. Builder's risk insurance insures against the risk including _____.
   A. physical loss
   B. property damage
   C. bodily injury
   D. both A and B

3. Marine insurance covers the damage of _____.
   A. ships at sea
   B. ships in warehouses
   C. ships at the harbour
   D. cargo on ships

II. Translate the following paragraph into Chinese.

Automobile insurance, known in the UK as motor insurance, is probably the most common form of insurance and may cover both legal liability claims against the driver and loss of or damage to the insured's vehicle itself. Throughout the United States an auto insurance policy is required to legally operate a motor vehicle on public roads. In some jurisdictions, bodily injury compensation for automobile accident victims has been changed to a no-fault system, which reduces or eliminates the ability to sue for compensation but provides automatic eligibility for benefits. Credit card companies insure against damage on rented cars. Driving School Insurance provides cover for any authorized driver whilst undergoing tuition cover, also unlike other motor policies provides cover for instructor liability where both the pupil and driving instructor are equally liable in the event of a claim.

III. Read the text and answer the following questions.

1. What risks will the crop insurance undertake?
2. What factors will affect the insurance company to decide the rates of earthquake insurance?
3. What is the purpose of insurance company designing the Landlord insurance?

金融英語閱讀 Financial English Reading

Chapter Five: Financial Events

Reading Comprehension

The Asian Financial Crisis

(*dialogue*)

A: The Asian financial crisis was the most important event in 1997 and 1998. I am very interested in this issue. I want to have a discussion with you about this event. To me, I think the outbreak of the Asian financial crisis in July 1997 resulted from the interaction among various internal and external factors in those countries.

B: Well, I would say the deterioration of their economic systems is the fundamental cause while the attack from international speculators sped it up.

A: I think the inappropriate pegged exchange rate system played a negative role in this event. It is such pegged exchange rate systems that touched off the crisis. For a long time, the Southeast Asian countries had fixed their currencies' exchange rates. Competitiveness had been weakened because of continuous deficit in their current accounts while the US economy has developed steadily. Under such conditions, to maintain the pegged exchange rate increased the pressure of devaluation on their currencies and made them vulnerable to attack from international speculation.

B: I think another reason is the imbalance of economic structure in these countries. During their economic booming period the Southeast Asian countries had invested a huge amount of capital in stocks and real estate rather than in the pillar industries. Therefore when economic growth slowed down, that investment only brought about larger quantities of dead and uncollectible accounts.

A: Excessive dependence on overseas loans also contributed a lot to the crisis. For a long time, the Southeast Asian countries had depended excessively for their economic development on overseas loans, especially short-time loans, which brought to them a tremendous interest burden. At the same time, in the Southeast Asian countries, nearly no single country had a fiscal budget balance.

B: In addition, I think the Southeast Asian countries opened up their capital accounts when they had not yet set up complete financial, taxation and government budget systems. They had weak financial supervision on financial activities. The attacks from international speculators and the consequent capital flight further intensified the critical situation.

A: I remember the Mexican financial crisis in 1994. The main reason for the crisis was rapid trade liberalization and inappropriate foreign investment policy. I find that there are several similarities between the two crises, such as huge deficit in current account, inappropriate foreign investment policy, excessive dependence on foreign loans especially short-time loans, inappropriate foreign exchange policy, excessive opening up of financial markets, imbalance of economic structure and so on.

B: But there still remain some differences between them. I think the Asian financial crisis resulted from the deterioration of the internal economy and financial crisis was speeded up by external attacks. However, in Mexico, it was the economic panic and the consequent capital flight that resulted from Mexico's default to its due debts that caused the financial crisis. Compared with the Mexican crisis, the Asian financial crisis has spread more widely and lasted longer.

A: What do you think we can learn from the Asian financial crisis?

B: I think the most important lesson is that economy and financial are closely linked. In order to maintain a sound economy so as to guarantee financial stability we have to do a lot of work. Fist of all, we should adhere to the reform and opening up policy. We should maintain a stable political situation and high lever confidence in China's economic development. Second, we should maintain continuous development of the national economy at a moderately rapid lever, improve the economic structure and increase the investment in infrastructure construction to support economic development. In addition, we should also speed up the reform of state-owned enterprises and enforce the macro-control and guard against the bubble economy.

A: Yes, and at the same time, we should also take efforts to improve China's financial area.

B: For example, I think we should adhere to a moderately tight financial and monetary policy. We should enforce financial supervision to guard against risks. On the other hand, we should speed up the transition of state-owned commercial banks to become real market-oriented commercial banks. Finally, we should open up the capital account gradually only when conditions permit and we should improve the foreign trade structure and maintain the balance in current accounts.

A: Well, we have discussed a lot about the crisis, but I still have a question. Since the outbreak of the Asian financial crisis in July 1997, the international community and the crisis-stricken countries have taken many measures to overcome the crisis. However, the Asian financial market is still in turmoil. What are the main reasons for that?

B: I think first of all, the slow and even negative economic growth caused by the crisis has hampered stability in Asia. Second, the devaluation of currencies has increased the debt burden for those enterprises in the crisis-stricken countries and accordingly reduced their production. Third, with the sharp increase in dead and uncollectible debts, banks in those countries have still been trapped in the plight.

A: Why is China safe from the economic crisis in Asia?

B: China enjoys a stable political situation and achieves continuous surplus in its current and capital accounts. Besides, China's foreign debts are mainly long-term loans and China possesses up to US $ 140 billion in foreign exchange reserves. This offers China strong resistance to the economic crisis. At the same time, China has not opened up its capital account and has still imposed strict restriction on the inflow of hot money. However, it does not mean that there exist no problems in China's financial field. The problems related to debts owned by state-owned enterprises to state-owned commercial banks has been quite serious. The transition for sate-owned commercial banks to become genuine market-oriented commercial banks has made very slow progress.

New Words and Expressions

London Inter-bank Offering Rate	倫敦銀行同業拆借利率
devaluation	n. 貨幣貶值
vulnerable	adj. 脆弱的，易受攻擊的
excessive	adj. 多餘的
default	adj. 未履行任務或責任
crisis	n. 危機

confidence	n.	信心
enterprises	n.	企業
bubble economy		泡沫經濟

Notes

1. Exchange rate: The exchange rate refers to the price of one currency expressed in terms of another. And there are two marked price methods. They are direct and indirect methods.

2. Spot exchange rate: Spot exchange rates are rates that are quoted for spot transaction of foreign exchange. Spot transactions usually require delivery of the exchange involved within two business days.

3. Forward exchange rates: They are fixed at the time the contract is opened and the contract is firm and binding upon both parties' delivery or sale at an agreed time in future.

Exercises

I. Choose the best answer to the following questions.

1. Which currencies use indirect marked price method?

    A. GBP.

    B. AUD.

    C. NZD.

    D. All of the above.

2. What is the main reason for the Mexican financial crisis in 1994?

    A. Rapid trade liberalization.

    B. Excessive dependence on foreign loans.

    C. Huge deficit in current account.

    D. Rapid development.

II. Translate the following sentences into Chinese.

1. The inappropriate pegged exchange rate system played a negative role in this event. It is such pegged exchange rate systems that touched off the crisis. For a long time, the Southeast Asian countries had fixed their currencies' exchange rates. Competitiveness had been weakened because of continuous deficit in their current accounts

while the US economy has developed steadily.

2. We should enforce financial supervision to guard against risks. On the other hand, we should speed up the transition of state-owned commercial banks to become real market-oriented commercial banks. Finally, we should open up the capital account gradually only when conditions permit and we should improve the foreign trade structure and maintain the balance in current accounts.

III. Read the text and answer the following questions.

1. Which marked price method does euro use?
2. Which characteristics does foreign exchange have?
3. Which factors decide the change of exchange rate?

Why the Bundesbank Is Wrong

By Martin Wolf

How far has the euro-zone come towards resolving its crisis? The optimistic answer would be that it has rescued itself from a heart attack, but must still manage a difficult convalescence, with a good chance of further attacks. It must also adopt a regime able to protect itself against future crises. This task, too, is incomplete. But the euro-zone has secured time. The big question is how well it now uses it.

Arguably, the crucial step is to agree on the nature of the illness. On this, progress is now being achieved, at least among economists. It is widely accepted that the balance of payments is fundamental to any understanding of the present crisis. Indeed, the balance of payments may matter more in the euro-zone than among economies not bound together in a currency union. Hans-Werner Sinn of CESifo, in Munich, has done much to explain, in his words, that 「the European Monetary Union is experiencing a serious internal balance of payments crisis that is similar, in important ways, to the crisis of the Bretton Woods System, in the years prior to its demise.」 A special issue of the CESifo Forum, published in January 2012, is dedicated to this theme. In March, Bruegel, a Brussels-based think-tank, published a seminal paper on 「Sudden Stops in the Euro Area」. Then, in late March, Jens Weidmann, president of the Bundesbank, explored the issue in a speech in London on 「rebalancing Europe」.

In the years of euphoria prior to the financial crisis, private capital flowed freely, not least into countries in southern Europe. Greece, Portugal and Spain ran current account deficits of 10 percent of gross domestic product, or more. These financed huge excesses of spending over income in private sectors, public sectors, or both. These economic booms also generated large losses in external competitiveness.

Then came the「sudden stops」in private inflows. As the Bruegel paper notes, such stops occurred during the global crisis of 2008 (affecting Greece and Ireland), in the spring of 2010 (affecting Greece, Ireland and Portugal) and, finally, in the second half of 2011 (affecting Italy, Portugal and Spain). In some cases, what happened went beyond a mere stop in inflows. Ireland, for example experienced large capital flight. Of course, when capital ceased to flow to the private sector, activity collapsed and the fiscal position worsened dramatically.

The euro-zone was unprepared for such an interruption in cross-border finance: it was believed impossible. Once the stops had happened, the euro-zone had two options: force external adjustment on countries shut out of the markets or finance them via official sources. The second was the chosen option, with the European Central Bank the dominant source of finance, in its role as lender of last resort to banks. The ECB has become the「European Monetary Fund」.

So what is to be done? Mr Weidman describes what he calls a「typical German position」. This is that「the deficit countries must adjust. They must address their structural problems. They must reduce domestic demand. They must become more competitive and they must increase their exports.」

What, in this, is the role of the surplus countries? On this, Mr Weidmann is clear:「it is sometimes suggested that rebalancing should be undertaken by「meeting in the middle', that is by making surplus countries such as Germany less competitive. This suggestion implies that the adjustment as such would be shared between deficit and surplus countries. But the question we have to ask ourselves is:「where would this take us? How can Europe succeed if we give up our hard-won competitiveness?」To succeed, Europe as a whole has to become more dynamic, more inventive and more productive.」

Alas, these remarks confuse productivity with competitiveness. Yet these are distinct: the US, for example, is more productive, but less competitive, than China. External competitiveness is relative. Moreover, at the global level, the adjustment must also be shared. Mr Weidmann knows this. As he says,「of course, surplus countries will eventually be affected as deficit countries adjust.」The question is by what mechanism.

The external competitiveness of the euro-zone depends on the exchange rate. Yet that is not a policy variable. Members can only seek to improve their competitiveness vis-à-vis one another. That is exactly what Germany did in the 2000s. Now this must be reversed. Goldman Sachs has provided two excellent pieces of research on what this might imply (「Achieving fiscal and external balance」, March 15 and 22). It concludes that, to achieve a sustainable external position, Portugal needs a real depreciation of its exchange rate of 35 per cent, Greece one of 30 per cent, Spain one of 20 per cent and Italy one of 10 ~ 15 per cent, while Ireland is now competitive. Such adjustments imply offsetting appreciation in core countries. Moreover, with average inflation of 2 per cent in the euro-zone and, say, zero inflation in currently uncompetitive countries, adjustment would take Portugal and Greece 15 years, Spain 10 years and Italy 5 ~ 10 years. Moreover, that would also imply 4 per cent annual inflation in the rest of the euro-zone.

Might such an internal adjustment even occur naturally? Yes, it might. At present, the ECB is pursuing an expansionary policy. At the same time, German banks surely want to lend more at home. A huge lending boom in Germany would be a big help. But suppose that did not happen. Then today's austerity-blighted euro-zone would end up with a prolonged period of weak demand. It might, as a result, generate a large shift in its net exports. For the rest of the world, that would be a beggar-my-neighbour policy, impossible to tolerate in hard times. For the euro-zone to pursue such a policy, while asking outsiders to increase their finance of its members in difficulty, via additional resources for the International Monetary Fund, would add insult to injury. The outsiders should just say no. They should insist, instead, that additional support must be predicated on two-sided adjustment inside the zone.

The good news is that agreement is emerging on the role in the crisis of the payments imbalances. The bad news is that the euro-zone does not yet agree that competitiveness is necessarily relative. As soon as it does, the route to convalescence will at least be clear, however hard.

New Words and Expressions

convalescence   *n.* 康復

Bundesbank	德意志聯邦銀行（德國央行）
regime	*n.* 機制
European Monetary Union	歐洲貨幣聯盟
dominant	*adj.* 占優勢的，統治的，支配的
demise	*n.* 死亡，終結
deficit	*n.* 不足額，赤字，虧空，虧損
surplus	*n.* 剩余額，順差，盈余
balance of payment	國際收支平衡
mechanism	*n.* 機制，機能
inflation	*n.* 膨脹；通貨膨脹
beggar-my-neighbour policy	損人利己政策

Notes

1. Euro-zone: officially called the euro area, is an economic and monetary union (EMU) of 17 European Union (EU) member states that have adopted the euro (€) as their common currency and sole legal tender. The euro-zone currently consists of Austria, Belgium, Cyprus, Estonia, Finland, France, Germany, Greece, Ireland, Italy, Luxembourg, Malta, the Netherlands, Portugal, Slovakia, Slovenia, and Spain.

2. European Monetary Union: is an umbrella term for the group of policies aimed at converging the economies of all members of the European Union at three stages.

3. Inflation: is a rise in the general level of prices of goods and services in an economy over a period of time. When the general price level rises, each unit of currency buys fewer goods and services.

4. International Monetary Fund: is an international organization that was initiated in 1944 at the Bretton Woods Conference and formally created in 1945 by 29 member countries. The IMF's stated goal was to stabilize exchange rates and assist the reconstruction of the world's international payment system post-World War II. Countries contribute money to a pool through a quota system from which countries with payment imbalances can borrow funds temporarily.

Exercises

I. Choose the best answer to the following questions.

1. About the current condition of the euro-zone crisis, which of the following statements is correct?

   A. The euro-zone has temporarily survived itself from the crisis.

   B. The euro-zone is under convalescence now.

   C. There can be further crisis.

   D. All of the above.

2. 「Arguably, the crucial step is to agree on the nature of the illness.」According to the passage, what is the nature of the illness?

   A. The incompetency of the European Central Bank.

   B. The imbalance of payment.

   C. The collapse of the Bretton Woods System.

   D. The lack of eurobonds

3. What did Mr. Weidmann suggest countries that is under crisis do?

   A. Mr. Weidmann suggested they spend less and export more.

   B. Mr. Weidmann suggested they expand their domestic demand.

   C. Mr. Weidmann suggested they borrow from the European Central Bank.

   D. Mr. Weidmann suggested they depreciate their currency.

4. While the author didn't agree with Mr. Weidmann's suggestion, what was the author's suggestion?

   A. The author suggested the establishment of the 「European Monetary Fund」.

   B. The author suggested that the ECB should pursue an expansionary policy.

   C. The author suggested the deficit countries depreciate their currency while surplus countries appreciate their currency.

   D. The author suggested Europe beg the help of outside economy like the US and China.

II. Translate the following sentences into Chinese.

1. It concludes that, to achieve a sustainable external position, Portugal needs a real depreciation of its exchange rate of 35 per cent, Greece one of 30 per cent, Spain

one of 20 per cent and Italy one of 10 ~ 15 per cent, while Ireland is now competitive. Such adjustments imply offsetting appreciation in core countries.

2. At present, the ECB is pursuing an expansionary policy. At the same time, German banks surely want to lend more at home. A huge lending boom in Germany would be a big help.

III. Read the text and answer the following questions.

1. What is the function of the balance of payment?

2. Why didn't the euro-zone prepare for such an interruption in cross-border finance?

3. What does the 「typical German position」 mean?

Greed Is Not Good for Goldman

By John Gapper

There are various ways to describe the synthetic collateralized debt obligation that Goldman Sachs constructed for John Paulson, the hedge fund manager who bet on the collapse of the mortgage bubble.

Goldman itself terms it 「nothing unusual or remarkable」. The US Securities and Exchange Commission describes the Abacus deal that closed in April 2007 as securities fraud. I call it short-term greedy.

Goldman rose to its dominant position on Wall Street through the dictum of Gus Levy, its former senior partner, that it should be 「long-term greedy」. He meant that it should forego quick gains for enduring profits.

The bank's expression of that principle on its website is: 「Whether a mid-size employer in Kansas, a larger school district in California, a pension fund for skilled workers, or a start-up technology firm, our clients' interests come first.」 So what about a Düsseldorf bank?

In late 2006, after an internal debate on its mortgage desk, Goldman made a farsighted decision to protect itself from what it had come to fear would be a severe downturn in the housing market. It pulled back from taking risk and hedged its mortgage book, saving itself from the deluge.

At exactly the same time, it was approached by Paulson & Co to structure a CDO that the hedge fund could make money by shorting. Paulson offered it a $15m fee to assemble the deal and find an investor that would take the risk from which Goldman was simultaneously fleeing.

Fabrice Tourre, Goldman's front-man on the deal, went to IKB, a bank that had invested in several of its Abacus CDOs and was a valuable Goldman client. He offered it a package, which it took without looking closely enough at the dodgy mortgage swaps inside.

When the smoke cleared, Paulson made a profit of about ＄1bn while IKB lost ＄150m and had to be bailed out that August. ACA Capital, which selected the securities, lost ＄900m and later failed (with ABN-Amro assuming liability). Goldman, which tried to shed its position but could not hedge it exactly, lost ＄100m.

The SEC will find it difficult to make a charge of fraud stick against Goldman and Mr Tourre. IKB was a 「qualified」 professional investor that was not supposed to need its hand held by an investment bank (although there always seems to be a German bank in such cases, eager to blow a hole in its balance sheet).

But judged by Levy's dictum, and the principles of John Whitehead, another senior partner (「We are dedicated to complying fully with the letter and spirit of the laws, rules and ethical principles that govern us. Our continued success depends on unswerving adherence to this standard」), Abacus was a tawdry episode.

None of the deal documents made clear that Paulson had called the tune and Goldman had initially acted on its behalf. Goldman has been reduced to brandishing the letter of the law and insisting that it adhered to 「market practice」, which is not the same as ethical principle.

Goldman gave 8m documents to the SEC, but did not include the overarching philosophy that brought it to Abacus, the strategy laid out by Lloyd Blankfein, its chairman and chief executive, in 2005.

As Charles Ellis's the Partnership records, Mr Blankfein feared that if Goldman stuck to its traditional separation of agency and principal businesses – keeping its client advisory and asset management work isolated from risk-taking with its own capital – it would be overtaken by commercial banks.

「Its complex variety of many businesses was sure to have lots of conflicts,」 Ellis writes. 「Goldman Sachs, Blankfein said, should embrace the challenge of those conflicts.」 It definitely embraced them with Abacus, keeping IKB in the dark both about Paulson and its own view of mortgage CDOs.

Goldman was, to borrow words from Robert Armstrong, the former British cabinet secretary, being 「economical with the truth」. It treated IKB like a trade counterparty while Paulson got the privileges associated with a client. The biggest client business in banking is mergers and acquisitions and there is a saying in M&A, honored more in the breach than the observance. It is that the best piece of advice a banker can give a client is not to do an ill-advised deal although he would earn a fee.

IKB was Goldman's client for its first Abacus deal in 2004, and, if it had truly put IKB first Goldman would have told it not to take part in the last one. Even as it was being assembled, Jonathan Egol, Mr Tourre's colleague, was e-mailing: 「You know I love it, all I'm saying is that the CDO business is dead and we don't have a lot of time left.」

Goldman can argue, and it does, that it did not have any fiduciary duty to IKB to tell it any such thing. It had a view of the mortgage market, IKB had another and Paulson & Co a third. They were all consenting counterparties operating in a sophisticated market.

In the end, that is not good enough, certainly not for a bank that takes pride on putting clients first. IKB was such one but, when it came to this deal, Goldman's message was: 「We're taking care of our balance sheet and you're on your own.」

Emanuel Derman, a former partner who was one of Goldman's first derivatives wizards, wrote on his blog this week: 「The SEC may be trying to cure unethical behaviour by treating it as illegality.」 But the law is all the SEC has; ethics are Goldman's responsibility.

New Words and Expressions

collateralize	v. 以⋯⋯作抵押
hedge fund	對沖基金
fraud	v. 詐欺, 詐騙
enduring	adj. 持久的, 不朽的
flee	v. 逃走, 逃避
unswerving	adj. 堅持不懈的, 堅定不移的
adherence	n. 遵守, 遵從
tawdry	adj. 華而不實的

conflict	*n.*	衝突；戰鬥；相互干擾
behalf	*n.*	方面，利益
fiduciary	*v.*	基於信用的，信託的，受信託的
mergers and acquisitions		企業併購

Notes

1. Goldman Sachs: is an American multinational investment banking firm that engages in global investment banking, securities, investment management, and other financial services primarily with institutional clients.

2. Hedge funds: are private, actively managed investment funds. They invest in a diverse range of markets, investment instruments, and strategies and are subject to the regulatory restrictions of their country. U.S. regulations limit hedge fund participation to certain classes of accredited investors.

3. Mortgage: is a loan secured by real property through the use of a mortgage note which evidences the existence of the loan and the encumbrance of that realty through the granting of a mortgage which secures the loan.

4. Counterparty: is a term most commonly used in the financial services industry to describe a legal entity, unincorporated entity or collection of entities to which an exposure to financial risk might exist. The word became widely used in the 1980s, particularly at the time of the Basel I in 1988. Sometimes it used instead of unicorporation. The legal entity notion is using as counterparty.

5. Mergers and acquisitions: is an aspect of corporate strategy, corporate finance and management dealing with the buying, selling, dividing and combining of different companies and similar entities that can help an enterprise grow rapidly in its sector or location of origin, or a new field or new location, without creating a subsidiary, other child entity or using a joint venture.

Exercises

I. Choose the best answer to the following questions.

1. Which of the following statements about IKB is NOT true, according to the article?

   A. IKB is a bank that had invested in several of its Abacus CDOs.

   B. IKB lost $150m and had to be bailed out.

C. IKB was a qualified investor that was not supposed to need its hand held by an investment bank.

D. IKB was treated like a privileged client by Goldman.

2. What's the author's attitude when he mentions the principle on Goldman's website in the 4th paragraph?

A. Strongly opposed.

B. Sarcastic.

C. Satisfied.

D. Nonchalant.

3. Which of the following is Goldman's actual behavior, according to the author?

A. Goldman seems to take care of only their balance sheet.

B. Goldman argues that it did not have any fiduciary duty to IKB to tell it any 「unnecessary message」.

C. Goldman treats IKB and Paulson differently.

D. All of the above.

4. According to the article, which of the following is TRUE?

A. The best piece of advice a banker can give a client should be based on whether he would earn a fee or not.

B. Gus Levy suggested that Goldman should seek for 「long-term greedy」.

C. The SEC will find it easy to make a charge of fraud stick against Goldman.

D. All of the above.

II. Translate the following sentences into Chinese.

1. The SEC will find it difficult to make a charge of fraud stick against Goldman and Mr Tourre. IKB was a 「qualified」 professional investor that was not supposed to need its hand held by an investment bank.

2. The biggest client business in banking is mergers and acquisitions and there is a saying in M&A, honored more in the breach than the observance. It is that the best piece of advice a banker can give a client is not to do an ill-advised deal although he would earn a fee.

III. Read the text and answer the following questions.

1. What dose the 「long-term greedy」 mean?

2. Who is the biggest client business in banking?

金融英語閱讀 Financial English Reading

A Possible Third Way for Bank Investors

Patrick Jenkins

  It is a long time since investors in European banks had much to cheer about. First-quarter results announcements over the past couple of weeks have done nothing to change that – profits remain elusive or at best depleted, dividends are minuscule or non-existent and share prices are still in a slump.

  That bleak investment case has been one reason why some annual shareholder meetings across Europe, as well as in the US, have been angry affairs, with big and small investors alike taking aim at generous pay deals for chief executives at a time of poor performance.

  Investors are right to demand that banks change their ways. But as I urged a fortnight ago, they should be taking issue not just with the perpetuation of stubbornly high chief executive remuneration but also with the pay bill for all staff. With the outlook for revenue and profit so cheerless at so many banks, one of the few other potential sources of funds for dividends is their bonus pools.

  There should be enough flexibility here to make the difference between a meagre payout and one that might even bear comparison to the halcyon days of 2005 or 2006.

  So far, especially in the US, investor pressure to find a dividend pot has focused instead on what many see as superfluous capital reserves, with persistent lobbying of both banks and regulators to return more of that 「excess capital」 to shareholders. As another previous column argued, the Federal Reserve acted prematurely in sanctioning most banks' plans to do just that despite the risk posed by the euro-zone crisis – one that is surely all the greater following the weekend election results in Greece and France.

  But what if there is a third way? One money manager, John Hadwen of US fund company Signature Global Advisors, is convinced there is. His idea is that banks and their regulators should consider a new structure for paying dividends to shareholders. The 「contingent dividend unit」 would be distributed as soon as a bank felt it could afford to make a payout, but the distribution could, in effect, be reversed if a bank's capital position deteriorated.

  The device is a new take on contingent capital, the long debated and as yet little used tool that some regulators believe should be an integral part of banks' capital structure in future.

In Switzerland, banks are implementing rules that will oblige them to hold contingent convertible bonds, widely known as Cocos, equivalent to at least 6 per cent of their risk-weighted assets.

The UK's Vickers Commission, appointed by the government to consider how to make Britain's banks safer, recommended last year that banks should issue as much as 10 per cent of risk-weighted assets in the form of Cocos or bail-in bonds on top of a 10 per cent equity ratio. The European Union is considering a similar plan.

But there are problems with both Cocos and bail-in bonds. Bail-in bonds are only really useful once a bank has got into significant difficulty and regulators are breaking it up. Cocos, meanwhile, risk being horribly ⌈pro-cyclical⌋ because they convert from debt into equity when a bank's core capital ratio falls to a preset level. That capital depletion would probably only have occurred as a result of steep losses, which would already have triggered a sharp fall in the share price. Sudden equity dilution in the form of Coco conversion would just make matters far worse.

Contingent dividend units, or CDUs, could be less problematic. The mechanism would be straightforward. Rather than getting a payout in cash, a shareholder would receive CDUs, which would be automatically put into a bank-managed fund that invested in low-risk assets. The CDUs could be traded in the short term, presumably at a small discount to their net asset value, but there would be an automatic conversion into cash after four or five years.

Signature has spoken to several banks, including Barclays and HSBC in the UK and Canada's CIBC, so far with no take-up of the idea. ⌈People think it's too radical not to pay a dividend in cash,⌋ says Mr Hadwen.

The main drawback of Cocos would, of course, also apply to CDUs because they would similarly convert into new equity precisely when capital reserves were depleted, diluting investors and compounding a share price fall.

But in the case of CDUs, the potential hit to shareholders would come with a key sweetener — rather than the contingent capital sitting on a bank's balance sheet; it would belong to shareholders, allowing investors to finally get an income boost after years of bleak returns. The promise of those payouts could also be an important spur to equity valuations at a time when so many banks' shares are still trading stubbornly at barely half their book value. Any idea that can help shake off that torpor – and not undermine the banks' capital strength – has got to be worth considering by banks and regulators alike.

New Words and Expressions

shareholder	n. 股票持有人
bleak	adj. 暗淡的, 昏暗的; 沒有指望的
depletion	n. 消耗, 損耗
deteriorated	adj. 惡化的, 已變質的
lobbying	n. 遊說
meagre	adj. 貧弱的, 貧乏的
superfluous	adj. 過多的, 多餘的
equity ratio	股東權益比率
drawback	n. 缺點, 劣勢

Notes

1. Shareholder: is an individual or institution (including a corporation) that legally owns a share of stock in a public or private corporation.

2. Federal reserve: is the central banking system of the United States. It was created on December 23, 1913, with the enactment of the Federal Reserve Act, largely in response to a series of financial panics, particularly a severe panic in 1907. Over time, the roles and responsibilities of the Federal Reserve System have expanded and its structure has evolved. Events such as the Great Depression were major factors leading to changes in the system.

3. Equity ratio: is a financial ratio indicating the relative proportion of equity used to finance a company's assets. The two components are often taken from the firm's balance sheet or statement of financial position (so-called book value), but the ratio may also be calculated using market values for both, if the company's equities are publicly traded.

4. Balance sheet: is a summary of the financial balances of a sole proprietorship, a business partnership, a corporation or other business organization, such as an LLC or an LLP. Assets, liabilities and ownership equity are listed as of a specific date, such

as the end of its financial year. A balance sheet is often described as a 「snapshot of a company's financial condition」.

Exercises

I. Choose the best answer to the following questions.

1. What does the 「bleak investment case」 lead to?
   A. Some annual shareholder meetings across Europe, or in the US, have been angry affairs.
   B. Some big and small investors alike take aim at generous pay deals for chief executives.
   C. Investors demand banks change their ways.
   D. A and B.

2. According to the passage, which of the following is incorrect?
   A. In the UK, investor pressure to find a dividend pot has focused on what many see as superfluous capital reserves.
   B. Persistent lobbying of both banks and regulators return more of that 「excess capital」 to shareholders.
   C. John, the US fund company Signature Global Advisors, is convinced there is a third way.
   D. The UK's Vickers Commission is appointed by the government.

3. According to the passage, which of the following is correct about bail-in bonds?
   A. It is used when a bank got in great trouble.
   B. It is used when a bank got into significant difficulty and regulators would break it up.
   C. It is used by regulators.
   D. All of the above.

4. In the case of CDUs, the potential hit to shareholders would come with a key sweetener, instead of _____.
   A. the contingent capital sitting on a bank's balance sheet
   B. the contingent fund
   C. the contingent cash

D. none of them is correct.

II. Translate the following sentences into Chinese.

1. That bleak investment case has been one reason why some annual shareholder meetings across Europe, as well as in the US, have been angry affairs, with big and small investors alike taking aim at generous pay deals for chief executives at a time of poor performance.

2. His idea is that banks and their regulators should consider a new structure for paying dividends to shareholders. The「contingent dividend unit」would be distributed as soon as a bank felt it could afford to make a payout, but the distribution could, in effect, be reversed if a bank's capital position deteriorated.

III. Read the text and answer the following questions.

1. What are the problems with both Cocos and bail-in bonds?
2. What is a possible third way for bank investors?

國家圖書館出版品預行編目(CIP)資料

金融英語閱讀/ 周婧玥 主編. -- 第二版.
-- 臺北市：崧燁文化，2018.07
　　面；　公分
ISBN 978-957-681-361-0(平裝)

1.商業英文 2.金融 3.讀本
805.18　　　　107011015

書名：金融英語閱讀
作者：周婧玥 主編
發行人：黃振庭
出版者：崧燁文化事業有限公司
發行者：崧燁文化事業有限公司
E-mail：sonbookservice@gmail.com
粉絲頁　　　　網址：
地址：台北市中正區重慶南路一段六十一號八樓815室
8F.-815, No.61, Sec. 1, Chongqing S. Rd., Zhongzheng Dist., Taipei City 100, Taiwan (R.O.C.)
電　話：(02)2370-3310　傳　真：(02) 2370-3210
總經銷：紅螞蟻圖書有限公司
地址：台北市內湖區舊宗路二段 121 巷 19 號
電話:02-2795-3656　傳真:02-2795-4100　網址：
印　刷：京峯彩色印刷有限公司（京峰數位）

　　本書版權為西南財經大學出版社所有授權崧博出版事業股份有限公司獨家發行電子書繁體字版。若有其他相關權利需授權請與西南財經大學出版社聯繫，經本公司授權後方得行使相關權利。

定價：300 元
發行日期：2018 年 7 月第二版
◎ 本書以POD印製發行